SONDER LIVES: HERE LIES SONDER LIGHT

DEDICATION

I dedicate this book to my parents: Ren Howlind and Gene Watkins. "Mommie-kins", thank you for teaching me how to always choose happy. "Father of us All", thank you for teaching me how to love to infinity and beyond.

In a non-awkward way, your love story inspired me to never settle; for a child who wanted nothing more than to feel love after a divorce, you succeeded in my eyes. And for that I am grateful. If I would have settled in this universe I would have never left California, traveled the world, or got around to finishing this book. I would have probably played it safe, continued living by broken rules, and never have gone to Burning Man.

Thank you for always answering my difficult questions as I continued growing curious in life, and for being there even when I go into a black hole of thoughts. I know it's not easy to explain to people what I've been up to, or why I choose to pursue certain ambitions in my life, so know how thankful I am that you never think me too odd to support unconditionally. You both rock out loud, and I am honored to be in your presence.

TABLE OF CONTENTS

SONDERLOGUE

Walking into an unfamiliar universe may seem oddly familiar. It's almost the same as your current reality, with a few adjustments in how words are interpreted. You've experienced this when reliving shared memories with someone you love. When engaging in conversations, and sharing how you felt, you realize that you both remember different versions of the same experience; same occurrence, but different versions. This doesn't discredit either party. It's simply an opportunity to expand on your acceptance that there are two different points of view.

These two different points of view are from two different universes. Let's start there. Everyone is their own universe, and based on where they orbit, they will see things slightly, if not extremely different from you.

In my universe, I began to understand this when I discovered a new word: *Sonder*. It was introduced to me on April 15, 2012, by Nathan Collins,

after hiking Cucamonga Peak in California, watching *Legend of Korra*, and being introduced to the graphic novel *Daytripper*. My universe was never the same. Sonder was a word coined back in 2012 by John Koenig, in a project called *The Dictionary of Obscure Sorrows,* which aimed to come up with new words for emotions that lacked words. Sonder is defined as the profound feeling of realizing that everyone, including strangers you pass in the street, has a life as complex as your own, which they are constantly living despite your lack of awareness of it.

Since seeing everyone in this new sonder light, life started moving forward. *CLICK*. Whether life *CLICKS* in alignment or *SNAPS* in disconnection it keeps flowing. Since this discovery of flow, the time has gone by in a *FLASH*. Memories will flood back instantly, and through reliving them, I get to review them emotionally. Many of these past memories you will revisit while reading this book. In 2015, September 6 to be exact, I wrote my first epiphany, one that echoes throughout this story: **Understand; And Hold onto this Key in the Universe.** Since then, through dreams, travel, and unforeseen conversations, this line still rings true.

Now, let's get comfortable with energy. Energy is all around us. It beckons to be used and used up completely, in hopes of becoming a new form of life. It wants to be all forms of life. Which types of life, you ask? Every type of life—people, plants, parasites, and pets. Now, this might be a stretch for some, but all energy is equal. And every bit plays a valuable role. It is known that energy cannot be created, nor destroyed . . . just moved. So throughout this story, from the point of view given by this universe, energy will be called *prana*. Prana is equal, regardless of where it resides in the universe: the sun, Mares or Arth. Yes, Mars is Mares, and Earth is Arth. This book modifies the hueman language as it would appear to a Maresan.

It's my understanding that some universal words are mixed up. I was taught that I live on Earth in the Milky Way Galaxy, but most prana beings of this universe call this planet Arth in the Reginald Galaxy. There! That isn't that much of a stretch. Take the Andromeda Galaxy, which is much older and the agreed to be the closest galaxy to us. The Andromedans think it's rubbish that huemans call the belaved Sir Reginald Star anything less than its regal title.

Oh . . . you might have caught that—*belaved*. Yes, Sir Reginald speaks from a language of *lave*. The word love is an evolved word from lave, similar to your word glitter evolving from *glister*. Just like prana, words can evolve. Take it up with Shakespeare sometime; if he ever comes back around, or observe this next time you have an argument. We see it happen when at least two universes are willing to come together and communicate with the intention of shedding light on previously declared dark words. This is exciting for those willing to wander in the wonder of what could be discovered in unknown worlds of darker words.

And that will take place very often in this book, which explores many different levels of communication that all prana have available to them. I used all four that I'm aware of, and I broke them down for you to aid you in your journey throughout this series:

1. When using verbal communication, "You will see it written in quotation marks."

2. When using telepathy, *"This will appear italicized and in quotations."*

3. When using internal communication, *<u>"This appears italicized and underlined. Unlike verbal communication or telepathy, it can only be heard by those who are part of the conversation—a direct line."</u>*

4. When Sonder uses inner intelligence, ***<u>"It appears bold, italicized and underlined. It is only to be used when having conversations with One's Self."</u>***

As far as this book goes, the main character will have a lot of self-reflection, especially while communicating with five very important pixelated prana beings. To keep track of them all, I have assigned them five different tonal patterns: Bass, Contralto, Baritone, Countertenor, and Soprano. And during this part of the journey, they are needed to shed enlightenment in areas of darkness; darkness that we desire to ascertain. When there is a desire to understand the darkness within one's own universal world, ultimately the pursuit leads to peace, and the ultimate freedom to pursue one's own happiness.

Again, I was fortunate to stumble upon this word sonder, and I'm elated to share what I gained through my experiences in finding my universal happiness in life, love, and the universe. I wish the same onto you through your Self-discoveries. So, without further ado, I bring forth Sonder Lives: Here Lies Sonder Light.

Places, everyone. It's showtime. *FLASH*.

SONDER LIVES

Here Lies Sonder Light

Part H

JANINE AYANA WATKINS

MIT — LIFE IS A GAME

You are about to embark on a mission . . .
in many, many words.
The mission is simply to live life. Life is simple.
There is only one thing you need to know.
Life is a game.

In this game, you can take any route. Not all
lead to victory, but do not be fearful of failing, or of
falling into darkness. With every restart, you are
granted a pair of fresh eyes, and sometimes old skills
acquired from previous games; never forget the
intention as to why you play. Your intention is to make
it through your unique labyrinth.

There are no shortcuts, and no one can help
you; they will only hinder you. It might seem helpful if
you seek them out, but within the labyrinth, prana
beings you encounter should be seen as walls or
walkways. Prana beings play important parts in our
labyrinths, reflections in living form, echoing messages
back to us that can give us direction. You play the
same role in their labyrinths, and we are all playing to

complete our games of life. Have fun with it, even if you come to find that a chosen direction is a dead-end or a distraction. Never be remorseful or unable to take a new path if a walkway is terminated, or leads you to a wall. Your Self already knows the way, so master the distractions as you begin identifying them, as they tend to repeat, often in looped, spiraled cycles. If you desire to get out of your cycle, you will.

Most importantly—and be honest with yourself—when beginning a new cycle, how do you most often choose to make moves? There are four choices: strive to ascend, strive to descend, avoid any movement, and trust every movement. The first three choices are trapped in an expectation on where you are supposed to go, but to trust in your process will always have you win your game of life. Prana beings often believe everything in life happens to them; a small, very powerful group, already knows that everything in life happens *through* them. This becomes easier to understand when you surround your Self with prana beings who are victors over their labyrinth walls rather than victims.

To practice, simply listen to all the different possibilities from all points of view. From there we will recognize that universal truth is made up of many different sonder lights all shining outwards from a topical source. These sonder lights together can enlighten areas previously filled with darkness and unknown fear. Exploring this darkness with the intention of trusting the unknown—instead of fearing it—illuminates the importance of understanding sonder lights; ultimately and intentionally, sonder light will alter how all lifeforms play this game.

Your intention is known by you the entire way throughout your labyrinth—even if you claim to not know it. Not choosing is also an option. So be mindful of how you choose to make your move. If you often find your Self getting frustrated about continuously being in a complacent loop, just think about what has you making the moves you do in your game of life. Focus and notice if your game has many repeated levels. The more misaligned you are with your intention, the more you will likely repeat recycled areas of life instead of exploring other missions.

And you know what? That's okay. This is your mission; your game. You get to play it any way you desire. It is your life, your lave, and your universe. So again, prepare to embark on a mission . . . in many, many words. This mission is Sonder's. Sonder Light's life is simple. *FLASH*l

1 HER NAME IS SONDER

"So. I am done."

"It's your choice," a deep and ominous voice booms.

"What's my choice?" *SNAP*. My initial thought disappears. Why am I holding this tiny glass tablet? *SNAP*. Did it just get dark? Was there even light to begin with? *SNAP*. What was I talking about?

"Are you done?" the ominous voice booms. A question with a question; that doesn't make sense. *SNAP*. What was I just wondering?

My mind is racing, and my thoughts seem to be falling away; the more I focus on this conversation, the more I forget. This is a perpetual catch twenty-two. Yup, the more I focus on remembering, the more I forget, but unless I focus, I cannot remember. I hear the tiniest voice: **_"Come back to your mission . . ."_** It drifts out of range. *SNAP*. I am slipping away.

FLASH. I ask, "What mission?" Wait. Was I just reading? Yes. I had something in my hand. What did I do with it? Was that a dream? Was I dreaming? A hear a deep-toned voice state, "Your mission." I

14

gasp! This voice is different than the previous one. The first voice sounded ominous, but this one sounds deeply grounded. How does he know about my mission? Was that a dream? Wait, no? Maybe not. It couldn't have been. And this deep, tonal voice who asks about my mission—maybe he can help.

"What was my mission?" My question is followed by silence. Then the bass-toned voice persists, "The mission assigned to you before you ended up back here." Okay, not helpful. Next time, I'll ask for a straightforward answer—relative to someone who clearly has amnesia. Wait, how do I remember amnesia, the concept of it, but not my mission or where I am? Have I died? No, I am very much living.

Darkness surrounds me, and the feeling of unwanted transparency and isolation while in the presence of this bleak audience. This stranger's familiar voice, my interrogating ally, asking for answers about a mission that is now unknown to me. Asking in a way as if he already knows the answer, which frustrates more than puzzles me.

Where am I, who am I? As I become more inquisitive, my awareness of my surroundings seems to engage, managing to filter through the darkness that hangs heavy in the interrogation room. I feel incapable of sight, and yet—little by little—a gradient of figures around the room come into my awareness. The inanimate objects consist of one table and two chairs; one of which I'm sitting on now. I conclude that there are a few living prana beings as well—however, they remain pixelated. I remain calm and continue to observe. Wherever we are, we are in a large vessel that is moving steadily. I shift my gaze all around the dark unit. The illumination increases and I focus on a convex window casting a silver-light lining, gifted by the stars themselves. I flush my being with relief that I am in space. *CLICK*. Huzzah! We are in space. Well, who is we? I have all but forgotten how this conversation started, and I am unsure of its context.

Wait, what was I wondering... oh yeah, where am I? This sterile, yet pleasant, oval room doesn't seem to be frequented much. This spacecraft appears to have two viewing windows that are identical in dimension and another window between them that is three times the size, almost wrapping the width of the room. I can see a little glint of starlight traveling outside of the vessel. Dim flickers of twinkle blink in and out of existence. How did I get here?

Looking around the room with different shades of gray present, I am curious why I do not see different hues. I choose to focus on something besides my lack of color spectrum. I reach down and touch the smooth and rounded lip of the chair I occupy. I gaze at the chair behind me. Why is this chair over here? Should it be close to the table too? Did I place myself here? I return my attention to my chair, which is more like a stool; it doesn't have armrests. As I watch myself touching the stool, I gasp. I failed to notice I'm pixelated! Wait; have I always been this way? No, I am supposed to be solid.

Comparing my lack of a defined right appendage to the smooth, finished chair, I become aware that the limb is somewhat transparent. I gaze across my entire being and see my other appendages and torso are compiled of random specks and bits. I hold up two of my left appendages and stare through them. Well, at least I'm still Maresan. *CLICK*. How do I remember Mares? I know I'm a pixelated Maresan with fractions of knowledge. I know I am alive, yet I'm not solid matter. I know of colors, yet I do not see them. I know of memories, yet my memory bank seems to hold nothing.

I dart my awareness upwards, and can now clearly see four pixelated figures scattered behind my bass-toned interrogator. They all seem to hover—I remain sitting. In conclusion, I'm one of six extraterrestrials in an oval-shaped room, all uncertain, but aware of a mission, and that's life. Or is it? There must be more. *CLICK*. There is! My awareness detects two corridors that lead out of the room opposite the wall of the viewing windows.

As I focus, I hear a great amount of commotion coming from beyond the passageways. The heightened sense of frequency out there compared to the frequencies in here is night and day. Their relative stillness is now alarming. What is causing so much frenzy beyond this room, and why are they not moved?

Why aren't they fazed? I know they can hear it—the commotion beyond the passageways. Yet . . . What could cause such a lack of concern for what is happening within their immediate universe? Could this answer they are inquiring of me offset the situation at hand that much—my mission? A break in my thoughts, as a voice in higher frequency than that

Bass character leads in. A baritone voice proceeds with the interrogation. "What is your mission, Sonder?"

Am I Sonder? *CLICK*. My thoughts—the me, the being whom I remember identifying as. Is it still Sonder? Yes, that feels true—but what mission? I look back and attempt to draw on collected memories. I cannot recollect any chain of events that occurred prior to me being on this ship as a conclusion of the aftermath of the explosion. *CLICK*. The explosion? Yes! There was an explosion—I did not survive. I died— *"You were the explosion,"* a new voice enters my head. Who was that? I gaze over and see one of the spectating prana moving forward as if they had spoken. Their tone was lower than Baritone, but it has a higher pitch than Bass, like a contralto tone . . . But wait. I didn't say anything—not even telepathically. Can they hear my—

Baritone humors me by continuing to speak, not that it is necessary, "My dear, we operate on a heightened level of communication and you also are capable of freely listening to the questions within all conscious minds. No questions are ever left unheard; you are capable of it too." Contralto swiftly adds telepathically, *"Apologies for chiming in. You just seemed to jump to descending thoughts quickly. I felt obligated to tele you."* A long pause, then Bass returns, "Give it some time. Like most skills, you seem to master things much quicker than most prana; and yes, the commotion outside of this room is because of what was manifested in your abrupt wave of dismantling your trinity being. Your physical and mental beings seem temporarily lost, but your spirit seems to be intact. And you might be satisfied to know that your incredibly noble sacrifice woke nearly half of the sleeping prana on Arth. An—"

I was relieved, "Did you say Arth?" I desired clarification and was given it by a voice higher than the three previous voices. A countertenor tone grabs my attention. "Ah. Perhaps your mental being is also intact. Yes, Arth. Located nearest to home planet Mares, within the Reginald galaxy. Now, please, we shall continue without further interruptions."

Bass proceeds, "We have observed much of the universe complete prana levels, yet very few have managed to have Arth accomplish its state of awakening, or reconnect to our universe. That's one thing that makes you fascinating." A tone in Bass's voice sounds proud, like a fanatic rooting for the underdog before they become recognized by others through a demonstration of their greatness. "You were favored starlight to be observed, since your completion of first level."

"Extraordinary performance, with almost no breaks from your first to forty-third level—" I interrupt yet again, "Forty-three? But we reincarnate after forty-two levels." No one contests. A few moments passed before the highest of all tones explained. The angelic Soprano asserts, "Well, Sonder. Your trinity went beyond that level limitation a few moments ago—before you exploded, that is."
Almost instantly, a hologrammed image of a young Arth woman is projected in front of me. I begin to tense up and lean back, but relax once I am certain it will not harm me. She has thick and curly hair

hanging about shoulder length, one side back. I cannot tell if the display is in color—it seems to be different shades of grey. I am mesmerized by this image, which appears to be so full of light and a fire that burns bright from her almond-shaped eyes. Nothing in particular stands out at once, although individually, all the features are remarkable. She wears the determined face of a warrior built with the stillness of a yogi.

As I look at her, I almost feel unworthy to be with someone so perfect. At the sight of her, I want to know more about her, until the instant that I think her too good for me. I scan how the other five seem to be drawn to her as well—all probably knowing more and being more useful to her than me. And then I get it. *CLICK*. She must be the reason I came back! I must not have been ready to leave her, almost like . . . a connection, or a calling. But why? What connected us? I become intrigued by this being. I want to drift next to her and gently nudge her to have her stir once more. Why won't she tell me why I am here? Why does she keep this secret to herself?

I look back to the others and crouch down in my stool. They probably told her I do not belong, because I cannot remember, and I do not fit in. I look back at her and know that it wouldn't matter. I can feel her radiant glow of acceptance. I do not need to know my past, because, with her, I could start a new future, one with color, and fresh memories; all things.

As I finally take in the essence of this creature, Soprano concludes, "She's astonishing—mentally, physically, and spiritually. Her name is Sonder, and you are quite aware of it." A massive hologram sun pops up, a few planets, and multiple tiny stars between me and the five of them. It touches the floor and rises up to the ceiling. Then the image of the woman dwarfs down to a falcon-egg-sized version of itself. It floats to the Arth that is nested within the hologram galaxy.

Countertenor picks it back up, "Most were terrified to see such a promising starlight jump to this radical type of behavior." A flicker goes off on the surface of Arth, and the egg-sized Sonder launches off of Arth, shoots beyond Mares and Fenuis, headed directly toward the sun. *CLICK*. This flickering motion grants me the sight of primary colors! I watch as it ripples throughout this room. I look around the room, then back at the hologram. I can see hues of blues, yellows, and reds. Can I see colors again?

"Sonder," Countertenor instructs, "lend your attention again to the astonishing performance as your prana hurls itself out of Arth's orbit, then shot through space, jet-set on a direct path toward the sun." I continue to watch in hopes of remembering what I was thinking, but become too distracted by the mesmerizing swirls of marbled colors I can see from all the magnificent, turning, spherical planets. Countertenor demands, "Sonder, focus. Now, what you'll see did happen to an extent; although it is the only thing that is being portrayed as true around the Universal Nation." As I watch the hologram continue toward the sun, I see a glitch-like glint within the stream, and then the hologram Sonder is quickly within the solar flares, and engulfed by the laps of fire.

A few moments pass by, and then I hear Soprano, "Let's see that again, but relative to the speed at which *you felt* you were traveling." The hologram refreshes, and I focus my attention on the egg-sized Sonder. She seems to be gliding with intention, not shooting erratically through space. At the same place I had witnessed that glitch-like glint within the stream, before she even comes close to Mares, now appears like a slow burning magnesium-strip. It's so bright, I wince.

Just then, I noticed an oval-shaped ship come into my awareness, behind the right-side of the egg-sized Sonder hologram. Her direct course to the sun is brought to a halt; then her size is dwarfed to a fraction of what it was, and her course immediately alters 123 degrees to the ship. *To this ship.*

With the satisfying conclusion of how the whole ordeal took place, Contralto explains, "Lo and behold, you disproved what all have led themselves to believe. What *you* did is not possible for others to comprehend. You deviated a set course without being acted upon by another external force. Their minds have betrayed them with a false image of you hurling your being into the sun. Because you did something outside of what they believe is physically capable, their cranium processor filled the rest based on the programming they have. You deviated your set course by acting upon a compelling internal force."

A brief pause. This has truth. Contralto returns—I hear a smile as she teles, *"You stopped, because you are still curious about this world."* I agree, but was there more? I still haven't a clue where I am, or the significance of these others in this room—or the others beyond those passageways. I practice telepathy, *"I recognize that I am Sonder, and I am curious about a lot of things—but I do not know what mission you're referring to."* Lucid-like thoughts will themselves to the surface of my memory, but they cannot make a clear appearance. I can faintly see them; I can sense they are images of familiar settings. It is almost as if I have awoken from a vivid dream, and can remember the sensation, but cannot recall what has just taken place.

I watch the hologram a bit longer before returning my attention to the room I am in. I chose to come to this ship—but why? All around this sleek and oval, canary yellow room. *Is there any significance to this spacecraft?* My attention is drawn back to Soprano who teles, *"It's quite normal for things to be a bit fuzzy now. Eventually, your set of unfinished lessons and incomplete experiences will drift back. Some of it will return as fragments, some as whole chunks. Everything you completed will not need to be revisited, rest assured. So beyond trying to remember what was, this is what is now. That is what is so."*

Bass tries to bring me back. "So, do you remember your mission?" I am reflecting on this question, which sounds more like a demand for information. A demand for information that I do not know how to retrieve. Again, I attempt to remember my mission; all I produce is failure. *SNAP*. I huff, "I—I do not have one." The tepid feeling within the room does not change, even though I become a bit hostile. Countertenor begins again, "Ah, Sonny-girl, will you forever have this universe questioning what you will do next?" I hear nothing they say following that name. . . *Sonny-girl?* I remember that endearing nickname! But how do they know it? Do they know me?

Stillness in here is maddening. I almost get madder, until I can choose to let go of the anguish that I'm working up. The moment I do, I feel a rush of relief, and I hear the five chanting on a higher frequency—a frequency I did not know was present. Was this how they heard me when I wasn't talking? Am I reading their minds? Their peaceful minds . . . It is quite soothing. I can still sense the anguish radiating from the room next door. I am still curious, but have more desire to stay with the soothing chants that I now relate with.

I'm not certain, but I feel that my prior Self would have chosen to leave this calming room for the more chaotic room. Presently, this suits me. I haven't a clue how long the other five have been in this state of being on this unknown level of life. And it shall remain unknown. I evaluate my surroundings. As I look around once more, I begin to recognize a sign stating: Main Lesson Capsule. *CLICK*. This is the Spacer Training Facility, which I was not to return to until I had completed the mission. Yes! I remember this was to transport me back home once I completed . . . . Drats.

These clouded memories are like the lucid dreams I'm trying to remember. They continue to almost break through the surface, but plunge back beneath before I can grasp their true meaning. I know it is there. My mission, my reason, my intention for this reality. I try to remember again, and I recognize the sleek and narrow circular layout of my belaved ship with more appreciation. I have now made the tie to my genesis before this forty-third level.

I chose to return to this ship, because it is mine. Is it still? I'm curious about the previous level I just completed. Do I have these memories? Are they still there, were there others—*Ariyan!* *CLICK*. I blurt out, "I had—I have a sibling! My mission. I can remember now—"

With great enlightenment, I regurgitate my mission: "My mission, as a spacer, is to awaken the sleepers of planet Arth in the Reginald galaxy. I was assigned to the great awakening mission of the sleepers at Zero Zone 2045 A.D." *CLICK*. Wait. Wait, wait. Wait. What was Zero Zone 2045 A.D.? Soprano comes through, *"Radiant question . . . You know, your questions might expand on worlds unknown. Would you like to practice a bit with me? We could elevate this whole conversation—easily be channeling on a level known as internal communication. Just like"—*Soprano demonstrates—*"this."*

I begin to let go of trying to figure out what Zero Zone 2045 A.D. is about, and instead tap into the internal communication line, and all the surrounding hums and rustles cease. How does this frequency

25

completely drown out all others? I focus on Soprano. Nothing else *CLICK*. I begin to inter-com, *"Too many sleepers were being misdirected to only see the possibility of listless choice."* This inter-com sounds so weird; eerily isolating . . . Nope, not doing that again. *SNAP*.

Baritone sheds light, "They followed a funneled model: praise or perish—the sleepers were never equal to the ones above... if they believed in such a thing. And sleepers do not believe duality shares benevolence in all arenas. It's either good or bad; rewards or consequences." I lean in with, "But consequences are relative—it's their version of truth that gives it validity." Baritone comes back, "Aye, but it's not the truth for the fearful majority —known as the flat-Arthers . . . errr, flatterers." The pixelated prana begins spinning, waving their tentacles around. I assume it is Baritone as they continue, "Flatterers will preach what they themselves do not practice, and typically are the first to judge. Like a co-worker that talks highly of their clan, but despises spending time with them. Or the neighbor who boasts about how much money he makes, but cannot stand his job." Watching their pixels spin is nauseating.

A question looms in, "If you know all of this, why are you here?" I direct to Baritone, "Don't share this with me, remind those spacers about those panicked flatterers, so they can return to their lives and not worry about me." Baritone tries to make a point again, *"If it wasn't you, I assure you they'd find something else. Before your explosion, those Spacers spent their time comparing their situations to fellow spacers and the flatterers. You don't yet see any correlation between—"*

I snap back, "Well, I've only been here, so I'm just speculating. Based on what I pieced together, it sounds like all those out there are experiencing fear consequential to my explosion. I don't think I was manic, but I want to figure out what I was thinking— access my thoughts, and fix this. I'm going to figure this out. Until then, I will let them know I am safe, and that they shouldn't panic. I can show them I'm okay, by returning to my mission; I'd rather try that, instead of mocking their fear. They're probably just screaming in terror, not knowing if I was trapped."

CLICK. Yes! There has been a perpetual catch twenty-two, causing prana to be trapped. It was said that the Arthlings perverted their conditioning and disconnected transcendence beyond twelve levels when exiting Arth." Nothing is said in response, so I continue, "Spacers of the Universal Nation started becoming entrapped if they perished on Arth as well—no spacers are safe from the recycling planet! It was as if Arth was collecting prana and not releasing them." As I say this, it does not sound right. Was there another truth to this story? Bass asks, "*What then?*"

My memory is a bit fuzzy, but I can still sense knowledge pooling in. I responded telepathically, "*I was the explosion. I am certain, but I do not remember why I did it. From what you just told me, and knowing that I was able to transcend beyond the layer, I can only imagine that I challenged it. I* switch back to speaking, "But skin suits don't just

27

combust . . . So what about Zero Zone caused me to explode, and what did I actually want to accomplish?"

I finally gather my thoughts and I recognize, stating it aloud. "My prana came back to this ship. So that means there must be a hole . . . wait, did you all get the coordinates as to where I exited? Can we find that hole?" The room is silent, perhaps because this was obvious since the beginning of this conversation, and did not need to be said.

But it wasn't obvious; otherwise, we would not have an issue of entrapped prana. I speculate. "I gather, by me not remaining on Arth, there must have been a hole above zero-zone that I crossed through. I must have known this and successfully shot through it. Why can't I remember how?"

"Or . . . Maybe I didn't need a hole." *CLICK*. "Didn't I just fly through the side of this ship?" *CLICK*. What am I? A sharp pause throughout the capsule. Then the instructions again, without explanation, the softest whisper, **_"Come back to your mission . . ."_** *SNAP*.

"I already told you my mission—are you just asking the same questions, like—like hypocritical flatterers or sleepers? I—I admit." *CLICK*. "I'm asking all these questions, because I don't remember anything! I'm doing my best, so stop demanding so much from me." In a lighthearted counter-explanation to my response, Bass begins to speak, "Come now, Sonder. Do give your curiosity recognition. Better to ask than assume. And make no mockery of divinity; sometimes it wants you to relax and flow more than you do. Divinity connects directly

28

to you through your inner intelligence. It whispers to you simply to give further direction. You do not have to follow it."

What inner intelligence? Contralto chooses to proceed, "You are ready for this level. We all are; but only by understanding our curiosity will we succeed. I believe success in this universe comes from unwavering curiosity to discover truth in areas unknown; and now, there is a lot that seems unknown, and so much to explore— and rediscover. Do you understand?" I nod, hearing this echo so true within my revived pixelated Self.

I express mutual feelings, "Yes, I understand that, and I wish to discover universal truth for myself and others." They all agree, "And so you did." I did? Did I really? *SNAP*. Frustrated, I bark out, "Well, if I did, then how come I cannot remember how I did it?" "Because," all five say in unison with mockery, "everything completed will not be repeated; rest assured."

I fall silent on my stool. Bass reassures me once more, "Eventually, any unfinished lessons and incomplete experiences will drift back—fragments of your past lifetime, you have an opportunity to complete them if you so choose. The universe isn't perfect; just divine. Perhaps in completing what drifts back to you, you will regain connection with your higher self." I exhale. "And what if I cannot?" In a very chipper voice, Soprano expresses, "Well, as long as you doubt it, you never will. Rest assured, if you hold onto your worry, at best, you'll stay stuck right here!"

Very bemused, I respond, "So if I doubt myself—" Countertenor cuts me short. "If anyone has even a little bit of doubt when they begin to ascend to another level, especially when attempting to transcend, they will automatically get entrapped." Baritone telepathically states, *"Hueman thoughts are not for the weak. If they are not of a strong mind, they are easily distracted and filled with doubt, and they lose focus and follow anything. All should do well to remember that. We all do it."*

My memory is shooting rapidly—like opened floodgates after a flash storm. All these bits of knowledge funneling out into a lifelong soliloquy. I wish to share them with these similar-looking prana beings, but they transpire so fast. I brace myself by grasping the lip of the stool. I recall my last conversation with Ariyan, one that stops the montage of images quicker than lightning across a dry desert sky. I see his face, clear in the dead of night, as he stares up at me. As I hone in on his mouth, I can tell he is yelling at me! I squawk out, "Oh! I realized something. Something that changed my ways of— Oh! What was it . . .?" Eager to hear what caused the change, Bass prompts, "Focus, Sonder. What did you realize? What did you tell Ariyan? Where is this memory? And—"

He continues, but I go placid. There is something inside of me that wants to be known and it becomes dominant over the other parts of me that hopelessly search for answers. I know this now. My allies are trying to reach this inner me, but I feel as though I yearn to pull away. Perhaps their true intentions are to help, but I know not why. They want to know something that I figured out before ascending. If they were watching me, then why don't they know why I did it? Am I now hiding something away for safekeeping? I do not know what I discovered, but I intend on discovering it again. These beings are like me, and so I wish to trust them— eventually. But listening to them with my head doesn't allow me to follow my heart. This ship is mine, and it's calling me to adventure. *CLICK*. I shall regain my past through personal exploration. Alone.

I acknowledge that Bass is still talking, but I'm over this conversation. I stop him by announcing telepathically, *"You're interrogating the wrong Sonder. You demand answers, without answering any of my questions, I can easily think of why your Sonder left. Demand so much, yet give so little. This reality is more hypocritical than when guardians vicariously live through their offspring."* I assume my point has been made about this interrogation when no further words come in response. "I'm going to investigate this ship of mine," I declare.

I begin to rise from the round stool, sprawling my appendages forward, and calibrating my coordinates. My pixelated form is relatively weightless; it doesn't seem to float away, nor sink through the floor. The thin, layered electrons between my lower appendages and the marble-like floor exchange places with one another. The sensation is not unlike tiny pop rocks detonating on the tongue. Uncertain of these newly engaged sensations, I set my intention to exit out the second passageway with more light beaming out. I'm hesitant at first, but after the second rotation of motion, it's all a repeat.

I am altering my conditioning of normalcy. Pixelated prana is my new form. My new normal. My coordination is a bit off, and the landing of my tentacles seems more forceful than necessary. As I continue onward with each step, I wish to master grace with ease. Each step is a trial in my skill of mobility, balance, and finesse. Before I reach the first passageway of the two corridors, I take an extra-long slip and begin to drift. I realize I can glide. I can glide! Woah. Why would you ever walk, when you can glide? Oh, what wondrous enhancement to skim just the thinnest plate of atoms effortlessly. No true effort used besides the intention and motivation to propel your motion. I am moving in ways I never knew possible.

As I approach both openings, only then do I realize that all the commotion is coming from the first passageway. Once I pass by, I feel my inner self whisper, ***"First things first."*** Is this the inner intelligence that Bass was talking about? I do not rebel against it because I was going to choose the storm over the silence anyway; it did not need to be said. I reverse my meek glide back to the dimly lit corridor. As I enter the passageway and glide with intent. I pass the passageway threshold, and I can hear a few of them tele, between each other, "*Gliding already; in both directions.*" "*Clever little one. Always has been.*" "*I wish us all safe travels.*"

I almost stop when I hear the last remark, but I proceed. The passageway is dark, but I can see the end is brimming with light. As I go forward, the light that shines from behind me begins to fade. My allies do not follow, and I do not look back. Instead, a fond memory becomes present. I remember now.

2 TUNNEL VISION

FLASH. Without full comprehension, I visit the day of my birth. I arrived earlier than expected.

Cassiopeia and Apollo, my duality guardians, were still on their "Making a Difference" (MAD) voyage, collecting the emotional data of Arthlings. They were sampling the mindsets of prana within huemanity, hoping to reach a conclusion why certain sample groups of huemans do not demonstrate equality for all prana. Most sample groups seem promising with their production of crops and living alongside their lands. However, four Kemet groups have been discovered to be infested with superiority complexes and adopted slavery practices. Prana who were willing to enslave others were already enslaving themselves—physically, mentally, and spiritually. It was detected and rapidly expanding throughout Kemet, with the power to spread to all parts of the world.

Yangs and yins—errr . . . brothers and sisters were selling brothers and sisters with no remorse to balance or self-worth. This discovery of disconnect extended their stay on Arth until the night I arrived. While getting dinner in one of the villages, Cassiopeia went into labor. Apollo scooped her up in his arms and rushed through the grasslands toward our hovercraft.

Cassiopeia shuddered in pain as my premature exodus from her womb began. Without the comforts of their ship—I was coming out. Apollo heard her pleas to stop and laid her gently down in the grass, putting his jacket and shirt under her head for support. Under a bright, full moon, Apollo answered the call to separate me from Cassiopeia right into the warmth and security of his arms. I take notice and observe this in third-person.

Hovering above my newly delivered self, I realize the moonlight seems to dim and I am now cast under a large shadow. I turn away from Apollo and see a neon blue, whale-sized electrical cloud coming down from the moon. It is directed at us. At that same moment, I'm nestled safely in my yang guardian's arms, Apollo feels Cassiopeia frantically tremble as she points toward the moon and gasps.

I look down and see Apollo crane his neck in time to catch a glimpse of the irregular blue beam of light rushing towards the three of us. It's at least three meters in diameter, hurling down from the sky like a tsunami of light crashing down on the grasslands. As the bolt goes through me, I close my eyes and tense up. When I open them again, I'm no longer looking down on my guardians, but up at them. Not fully coordinated, but in my physical body, I am overwhelmed with emotions that surge from my tear

35

ducts. I'm aware of my place in the universe. Part of this seems unreal, as I look sideways at Cassiopeia. I can feel her warmth surrounding me. This seems like an unfamiliar sensation of nostalgia. I try to speak words and ask questions, but my mouth is incapable and my head is swirling with new images.

Memories ripple through me, whirls of faces and images, but none stay too long before they're whisked away. Instantly, questions come: ***"Who in this world am I? Where are the other pixel prana beings?"*** I see so many faces, hear numerous sounds, and try again to communicate; but within my own head, I only hear baby cries. My feeble tentacles try to grasp some of the pictures right out of the air and fail. I am now soothed in my struggle by Apollo's embrace as my tentacles wrap around his forearm. The pictures stop, and I become one with the hug. My questions are subdued, as Apollo looks into Cassiopeia's eyes, and then Cassiopeia looks into mine. I gaze back at her—still trying to communicate in vain, while tears blur my vision. I remember her saying, "This universe will never be the same."

Many moments lapse before I recall seeing Ariyan. I can recollect this interaction so vibrantly. His light olive complexion, slick straight golden hair hanging in his wide almond shaped steel blue eyes. His petite frame is swathed in an oversized, burlap-looking wrap. He came up to me, kissed me on my forehead, and while touching his forehead to mine, he beamed to me telepathically, "*I will protect you.*" I understood his complete serenity in the commitment of lave. I communicated back, *"Heartfelt appreciation, Ariyan."*

FLASH. Everything goes dark! And then—one circular light. I come out of the memory and experience a surreal feeling of tunnel vision. I jolt a bit, forgetting that I was gliding. I marvel as I realize I've been on this ship the entire time; I never left. Okay . . . so I don't really go anywhere when reliving memories. That was frightful not being able to communicate with others. I would have been lost if not for Ariyan. That must have been my first telepathic conversation. I stop gliding and really ponder. Why didn't my guardians communicate telepathically with me—out in the field? Why did they only speak to me? They must have known—did they not think about it? Or did they not think I was going to get it right away? Did they not think about—

Countertenor's voice teles, startles me, *"Great questions. Now, do you have any questions that help you move forward?"* I almost get angry—but stop myself from doing so. *CLICK*. He's completely right. I could keep asking questions that have me going in circles. But I am here to move forward. I was able to revisit that memory, because something from it was not complete. Based on what I saw, why wasn't it complete? What question would I have to ask to have it be complete? I—I— *CLICK*. Oh! I know what the question is: Who was thinking? It's obvious! Ariyan. Ariyan was thinking! Huzzah!

I feel so *CLICK* light. I feel so *CLICK* grateful. I am so grateful for Ariyan. Most of my initial levels I ascended exponentially, because Ariyan was pushing me to allevelate to evolve with mastery through my levels. He instilled my lave for asking questions, staying curious, and being present. Contralto comes back. *"Now, there might be another question to follow this one, one that may or may not come to you right away."* I give it a shot; close my eyes, focus, and . . . nothing. Drats!

I cannot do this. I'm just not *SNAP* ready. I'm wasting *SNAP* time. How do they stay so calm and collected? Maybe I will remember faster if I stay with them. They know what questions to ask. Perhaps with their help, I'll be able to get back to my mission sooner. I look backward. It's almost tempting, but this feeling of going back into my head propels my heart steadfast toward the opening. I shall remember through observations of self-reflection, and not just self-examination—keep my Self moving toward new lights and whatever I feel drawn to; ascend and transcend, I say. *CLICK*.

What if I am faced with adversity and disappointment that I cannot overcome? *SNAP*. I still have emotional ties to my hueman being, Susun; I can feel it. I take my Maresan form, but my huemanity still remains. Emotions are difficult. *SNAP*. Contralto inserts, *"Be mindful of your thoughts. The way you think directs your path."* I stop moving and take this advice immediately. They are absolutely accurate. I am channeling the hueman spirit, which is attached to unspoken magic. If I believe there's a possibility I won't overcome these difficulties, then abracadabra—look what I've got. I can take every leg of this journey with the intention of wherever I go, I trust in my flow. *CLICK*.

It's strange that hueman beings don't trust flow. Throughout history, they are notorious for not remembering painful past lessons, and would rather write over the difficulties than reflect on why the same destructive loops continue to repeat. It's no surprise why they all unanimously slowly slip back into sleep; history repeats as they reach for the snooze button. I cannot imagine what kind of brainwarshing has numbed this fighting hueman spirit from not growing restless after two centuries. It's time to wake them up. Is that why I did it? Why I exploded? Why can't I remember how?

CLICK. Ariyan. Ariyan was supposed to be the wake-up call, not me. Ariyan was a reminder to all in his wake that all Arthlings are supreme beings; all beings are brothers and sisters in their own representing skin suits. All are led by their own divine inner lights, which are larger than their limited physical lives. He was given the name after the late Ariyan, who restructured the Universal Network into the Universal Nation, and the universe was brought to peace through unity and trust. This was his purpose, not mine. I listen to the shouts grow in volume as I near the end. This is the result of my erratic behavior; it doesn't seem like peace was manifested, down there or up here. I am ashamed at how my actions have disrupted our core intentions and shattered the current set of believed truths. It's all my fault that we are probably set back even further than ever after what I've done. *SNAP*. I feel heavy. Oh, Ariyan—where are you now? I could really use your guidance.

Silence is the only response I receive. Remnants of Ariyan hang heavy in my heart. *SNAP*. I'm lacking security in my abilities to figure this out. I continue to glide forward and feel my confidence near its end like this tunnel. Nearing the opening of the passageway, memory serves to recall that all corridors lead to—yes! The Central Terminal; I'm going into the Central Terminal. From there, I will gain my bearings, and I could . . . I could. Where might I want to go? *CLICK*.

Ah-ha! I will head straight to my quarters. I am sure my belongings left behind will provide me with memories. This is still my ship, and I will succeed. *CLICK*. My boost helps me regain composure but doesn't hinder my caution as I approach the buzzing of this unmistakable hysteria; echoes of frantic and indirect panic. Shouts are blurted out with no real designated receivers, just impulsive spurts of uncontrolled prana. Gliding toward these maddening sounds coming from the supposedly elite minds of the universe, I cannot help but ponder what may come next. I pause and reflect—back toward the darkened tunnel from where I just came, it's not too late . . . I could let the pixel beings lead the way to rediscover my Self. What's there for me to discover newly? Baritone teles, *"Radiant question, Sonder Light . . . or should I refer to you as Susun Link again?"*

That doesn't answer my question, but it has me move forward, no longer looking back. I will rediscover my Self on my own. I respond, *"Whichever you choose; now let me be for a while."* I am granted freedom with an, *"As you wish."* I glide forward, intending to reveal my past, distancing myself from those who understand me currently. Does this feel right? I question my choice again. Standing there, looking inward, I quietly plead for a bit of inner guidance. Quickly, letting go of the desire to figure it out on my own, I wholeheartedly listen to see if I should either: stay stagnant in a room or roam a possibly enormous spaceship.

Is there any way I can know for certain which way would be best for me to go? No response; I guess I get what I ask for. I begin to glide forward with the intention to trust my flow. *CLICK*. As the universe would have it, I am gifted a memory. As it materializes, I prepare to be reminded of the most famous star to have ever found himself in a similar situation: to stay or to grow. I see the smiling face of Apollo as I slip into my favorite Self-Discover-Me story of the brave Sir Reginald. It is the longest-running tale told in all the galaxies, about the noblest bit of stardust to travel with divinity.

3 SIR REGINALD

FLASH. Apollo begins the story that was told to him of the Benevolent Sir Reginald Star, passed down from cosmos to cosmos, now sharing his own rendering—with an introductory jazzy 70s theme song.

He dims the lights, sings his jingle, and does the coolest moonwalk toward me before sitting on the edge of my resting unit back on our clan's hovercraft. He already has his storytelling voice engaged which leaves lots of anticipation at the end of each sentence, as if I do not know what already comes next. I grin as he rushes into my absolute favorite Self-Discover-Me tale.

Apollo begins, "Upon an unknown time," there was a young star that was birthed in the wrong galaxy! On the eve that starburst into existence, it flickered with emotions so great that the star immediately acquired intention, and in that instant, he knew he needed to find his true home among the cosmos . . ."

"Wait," I interrupt telepathically, cascading my front tentacles down to the floor. I try to glide, but I

am much denser in my solid-state. I make haste to reach the light switch by the doorway and turn it on. I have questions that need answering—and I am not going into deep REM just yet. "*A soul, in a star, with a sense of belonging; what does that mean? What causes a star to have the capacity to know—to feel it was out of place?*"

I intend on staying awake for the entirety of the story, so the light will remain on. Satisfied with my minor retaliation towards sleeping in my deep REM routine, I return to my resting unit. I reach my front tentacles up onto the side and experience difficulty pulling my gravity-dense body up. I struggle for a bit before Apollo effortlessly lifts my whole being and cradles me in his arms, before returning me to the exact location I was in before I turned on the lights.

Apollo has already morphed into his semi-permeable squishy Arthling skin suit. His dark-brown hair seems a bit longer than the night of my birth, and his oil bronzed complexion has all but faded to sun-bleached sand. He often wears a long-sleeved sweater during this phase of transition, so when he touches me, I will not become hypersensitive to his moist and very smooth texture. I might have been born on Arth, but as my memory serves, I refuse to adopt any hueman customs, especially vocal communication; telepathy is superior. My clan did not force me to practice, and since I had not been assigned an Arth body, there was no need to start. Life is simple, and I am quite content remaining in my Maresan natural form.

43

I do not remember what being hueman felt like, but I speculate that the functionality is not transferred over. Apollo, for example, was much more muscular as a Maresan. He is a galaxy-known titan: built to defend. His assigned Arth skin suit is only necessary to get in the hovercraft to drive—built to clean soda spills and rescue snacks from going uneaten. Ariyan calls it, "An American Dad Bod—burly, beer-bellied, blue-collared, typical tailgating guy with enough charm to get the hottest gal of his dreams." He never upgraded, nor did he need to. It looks great in sweaters and I lave his squishy form.

Apollo's jaw is slightly clenched. I know he's withholding a smile, and not wishing to entertain my not-so-subtle attempt to postpone my inevitable REM sleep, he verbally responds, "Sonder, my light, please let me—"

Again, I cut Apollo off. *"I'm just saying, it's a bit suspicious of a star to stray knowing everything is divine. I mean what leads a star to question if it's in the wrong galaxy anyway? Isn't that relative? If I—"*

I'm cut off by a voice echoing from the door frame, "Of course Sir Reginald could not start out where he was supposed to be. I mean, being a story with a timeless moral in the end, able to withstand the test of time, means not only does Sir Reginald have to be out of place, but he needs to feel this sense of displacement within himself. Otherwise, there would be no story, because it wouldn't be relatable."

Ariyan takes one step in, flicks his almost shoulder-length hair to the side, and dims the light. Before he does, I notice a drastic transformation of his skin suit. He's increased in height and muscle tone, which typically happens through allevelation; he's a growing yang. I am distracted by his new look, although I'm fully aware he's turning off the lights without asking. I look at Apollo for back-up, but he just shrugs. The lights stay dimmed. My attention goes to Ariyan, who has joined Apollo at the edge of my capsule. As I look at them both, I become very aware of how similar they both look aside from the hair color. Knowing that one day soon I'll be joining them makes me smile. For now, I am content being swayed to stay back by hearing my favorite transcendence story.

Ariyan eases me, "Sonder, all great stories have obvious conflict; this one is no exception." It's clear to me why Ariyan is ranked with the high potential as an emerging leader within Spacer University. He has yet to hit the requirements for recruitment, but it is expected for him to hit eligibility by the next Arth cycle. His understanding for purpose in all mental, physical, and spiritual beings in this universe is inspiring and light-years ahead of most teenage leveled prana beings.

"That is exactly it, Ariyan! Well said," Apollo acknowledges. Ariyan leaps back into the story. "Reginald was a bit hesitant of his feelings to head somewhere new, mainly because he'd never seen anything move. Stars seemed to come into existence and just dwindled out. In observation of the glistering twinkles all around him, all seem to have agreed to stay in their designated places of birth, until they no longer existed. Those who were more flashy or glistery appeared to diminish quicker. By all the lights and

45

lumps in the universe, it was observed that it would be better to move very little, and best to do nothing at all. But this only led Reginald to wonder, 'Why be here at all, if you are just waiting to see how long you can outlast the others around you?'"

Apollo continues, "Sir Reginald was no ordinary star. He had his doubts, but he could feel he had a true calling, and it was to prove to himself that there was more to this universe than safely waiting to perish. That is *why* he was born away from his home, which would persistently call him to return to his rightful place, and be a leader in action. Reginald looked out where his home was calling."

Ariyan inserts, "He saw nothing besides a vast, empty space, but he felt that it was worth everything to begin the unknown journey into darkness. He did not know what he was destined to experience, nor did he know how far away he would travel. He only knew that he was headed out of this current galaxy to the great unknown and beyond . . ."

"Nicely put, Ariyan," Apollo acknowledges.

They both unravel this story, one after the other. Apollo continues, "Sir Reginald glanced around, one more time. Never had he questioned if he should inform the others of his internal thoughts. Reginald was concerned that any radical type of movement might cause panic to ensue; but in the following moment, he witnessed a dimly lit star fizzle out of existence. It was horrifying to him! All the nearby glisters simply gazed in the direction of this long-lived star that no longer twinkled for less than a moment, before returning to their own perpetuated wait for the same conclusion. That was it for Reginald—he was not willing to come to this same conclusion. Nay, nay, nay! He was damned either way; so he chose to at least see where else his fizzle could flicker out."

Ariyan chimes in, "It was not as easy as it sounded. Sir Reginald was young, but he was also massive. He began to rock back and forth, with very little result. He then tried to flash brightly, in hopes of creating a reverberating pulse, which got the attention of all the lights and lumps sitting around him, but no other results. It wasn't until he began to spin that he created momentum for movement. He had never seen anyone else move, and he had no idea what it was like, but as he did it himself, he came to realize unfamiliarity is not a comfortable experience. It was a bit nauseating for him, to feel as though he was just going in circles, but not truly going anywhere. He thought after a few rotations he would stop, and give up . . ."

Apollo adds, "But best believe, he knew this was the right path for him."

With a great amount of enthusiasm, Ariyan jumps back in it. "Yes, he'd broken free from complacency! He realized he had not set an intention! He was moving side to side, but it wasn't until he declared he would go toward home that his rotation had him begin to project forward! He was certain he could get there. Little did he know divinity was about to strike; it would strike the uncertainty that lived within his own mind . . ."

Satisfied with a long enough pause, I jump in telepathically, *"Reginald's excitement soon turned into panic as the familiarity of his surroundings dwindled. As he traveled, certain lights and lumps, who were envious of his purpose, intentionally tried to get in his way, determined to stop him from continuing homeward. He began to fumble a bit, in avoiding them, lightly hitting soft debris, which would send discomfort and shock to his whole being. With every hit, more discomfort. After the first few knocks, he realized he was dissipating in size with every collision! He glanced back and saw shimmers of himself left behind as a faint, glowing zigzagging pattern. Reginald was new to moving—and worried he was making a mistake. For the first time, he became fearful to continue."*

"Hey, that's great, Sonder. You want to try vocalizing the next part, or may I pick back up?" Satisfied with my teled contribution, I lean back as Ariyan takes the lead, "Reginald was destined to go somewhere greater, but he was afraid in doing so, he would lose himself. Motionless, Reginald knew not what to do, and an overflow of sorrow turned into wallowing and wails. His waterworks left him covered in star tears, now frozen in streams on the outer shell. Oh, what a sight . . . But this was Sir Reginald! He reexamined his situation: fizzle out here, or keep going to see how far his flicker would fly. His bursts of desperation turned to redemption. Sir Reginald wiped away his remaining tear streams, and mustered up enough bravery and determination to keep moving."

Apollo put his hefty arm around Ariyan and proceeds, "Sir Reginald came into a cluster of occupied space. Taking a moment for self-reflection, he remembered where he was heading, his attention was drawn slightly to the left; still homeward bound. Just beyond this congested space was a vast ocean of blackness; no existing debris and nothing to collide with. He would have to travel through this very rough passage, in order to blaze a new path. With tenacity, he made his way through the space of existing lights and lumps, took a leap, and made it to the vast open space. He moved, freely and unapologetically."

Ariyan escapes Apollo's arm by scooting closer to me and bursts in, "He was now soaring at full speed, fueled by bravery through the great unknown—thrusting forward, willing to face anything and everything no matter what!"

Apollo chuckles. Peeking over Ariyan's shoulder, he adds, "Reginald now looked beside him to discover that he was not entirely alone. Some fragments of himself that he thought were left behind—"
Ariyan cuts him short with lively animation, "—were traveling in his wake!"

Apollo wraps his arms around Ariyan's shoulder, giving him a noogie. "Ha! It seems like you embody a similar amount of tenacity as these little fragmented bits, Champ." I giggle, as Apollo resumes, "It was *because* each glint has its own spirit. The glints of his stardust still traveled, regardless of their size. Spreading out in all directions, Reginald is enamored at the sight. Because he was willing to lose himself, his

49

fragments were now free to expand and fulfill in whatever they were destined to do in this empty space. Through his actions, other beings who observed his travels now related to him without previously knowing it!"

"Ancient celestial bodies that had not budged in a millennium were now flying," Ariyan emphasizes. "Not all willing to do as much, or match his lightspeed pace through the unknown, but they were moving. Some were satisfied enough by knowing that they could move without doing it, others felt accomplished by spinning a bit and then settling back in, and others began to follow Sir Reginald's pathway closely, if not exactly. Regardless of the impact on others, it was clear to Reginald that he was the cause behind this universal sea now stirring in his wake. Unbeknownst to him, by choosing to head into the unknown, he was headed for an incredible opportunity yet to be revealed."

Apollo dramatically pauses to enforce this point. He then winks, cueing Ariyan to continue, "A wave of relief rushed over him, because he knew no matter how far he traveled from his genesis, he would know who he was. Even in this unfamiliar place, he found comfort knowing he was the same star he'd started out as. He looked slightly different on the outside, but his core hadn't changed. He was still massive compared to those around him, but his new outer layer shined much brighter. He confidently zoomed through the darkness toward the feeling that called for him to come home, even though he was unable to see it, he intuitively followed the calling to his true spot among all the millions and millions of bright lights around him. With his course set, he continued to pick up speed, not knowing what was to come."

Apollo now resumed again, "Cruising headstrong into the darkness, it became clear to Reginald that he was no longer the only star blazing a trail in this unknown space. Approaching at a higher speed was a shooting star that needed no introduction. Now nearing an intersection with him was the sweet star named Lady Andromeda."

I interject, *"How did he know she was sweet if he'd never moved before? Had he met her before? What if she just wanted to bump him like the other stars?"*

Both Ariyan and I look at Apollo, who says with omnipotence, "When you know, you know."

Ariyan now nods his head like that ambiguous statement was clear. I dismiss Apollo's dubiousness as he continues, "Reginald said to himself, 'This starlight is brighter, bigger, and more bodacious than even me!' He knew he was meant to keep going, but for some reason, he lost motivation to move beyond their immediate intersection. It was as if he was now drawn to the glistery glow of this unfamiliar star—a pull so lovely and strong that Reginald directed himself toward the star's light. He grew lighter and warmer. His beams and glimmer twinkled and flickered in a magnificent display for all to see!"

Ariyan begins making noises with his mouth that sound like a flushing toilet, causing Apollo and me to erupt in laughter. Minutes later, still giggling,

51

Apollo picks back up, "As Andromeda approached, Reginald heard a faint hum. It was a hum so miraculous that Reginald could not imagine it ever coming from anything other than Andromeda. He wished to know of her warm embrace and to never leave her side. It was a desire stronger than any he had ever felt. He pondered, 'What if I were to match my path to hers? Maybe I could learn and grow with her in my life.' Once the thought was now manifested—instantly after it was spoken—Reginald couldn't stop himself from only wanting to live life with her."

Apollo looked right at me, reflecting back wild and curious eyes, "Reginald couldn't stop himself. He had almost completely forgotten about finding home, because he now had this magical opportunity to experience the powerful feeling that all prana hope to get a chance to experience. For those who have never felt this feeling, it seems absurd to defy divinity; but for those who have known this feeling, there are no explanations needed for not wanting to give it up . . ."

A firm, yet soft voice came echoing through the passageway, "Apollo, stop dragging it out." Just then, Cassiopeia emerges in a flowy, one-strap dress that cascades from her toned torso down to the floor in an array of multiple colored silks. She lightly pats her bundled, golden chignon bun of hair, which conceals her right ear. As if she heard my rebellious demands, she flicks up the light switch. Unlike Ariyan and Apollo's seasonal tans, she has a year-round olive complexion. She radiates beauty from the inside out. I glance at Apollo, who's wearing the unmistakable look of true and unconditional devotion to his belaved Cassiopeia; she reciprocates an alluring look as she steps into the room.

Just then, Ariyan springs up, and sprints to rest his head on the comfort of Cassiopeia's clavicle, wrapping his arms around her shoulders gently. Ariyan lifts his head, and reassures her, "That's perfectly fine, Cassiopeia. I have not experienced *it* either, but I lave the build-up in the story!"

Cassiopeia giggles with understanding. She replies, "Oh, my special star-bright, Adrian. I can hardly wait for the day you'll tell me that you have discovered this feeling." She playfully clasps her arms around Ariyan, lifting and spinning him around twice, "And it's mother, my sweet Adrian!" Both engage in a shared moment of glee. At the same time, Apollo looks over at me, and whispers, "Mother . . . Already?"

Once Apollo has brought it to my attention, I too wonder why Cassiopeia starts calling Ariyan Adrian, or refers to herself as mother. Since when did she use Arthling terminology this early? They usually wait until they're within the orbit of Arth, before using Arth-like greetings. Curiosity got me, "*Apologies, Cassiopeia, but—*"

She stops her playful moment with Ariyan, "That goes for you too, young lady. It's time you began calling me your mother. Because we're all qualified for Arth clearance. We are all going on our first Arth clan voyage!"

At this thought, my whole being vibrates, and I ecstatically tele, "*YOU MEAN—ACTUALLY? ARE YOU CERTAIN?*"

Both Cassiopeia and Apollo say in harmony, "Affirmative. It has been permitted." Cassiopeia cheerfully announces, "Forkins Clan Unit: Otto, Casey, Adrian, and Susun are go!"

I look at Apollo, who had not hinted to this knowledge earlier; he must have been stringing me along. I knew Ariyan was not in on it, because he genuinely was as shocked and delighted as me! After registering what she said, he looks at me, "Sonder—err, I mean Susun, this is stupendous! Congratulations, little sister." Ariyan and Cassiopeia come and sit between Apollo and me.

Cassiopeia playfully touches Apollo's forearm, and proceeds to ask, "Otto, dear. Do you have the morph orb?" Apollo gives her a side smile, and under his long-sleeve shirt, he presents me with a small, yet very dense indigo marble sphere. He holds it out to me, and gestures to take it, "For you, Susun . . . Skin sack or not, you're still my *Sonny-girl.*"

I giggle as I send my four front tentacles out to grab the morph orb. I knew what it was—my very own skin suit. Also called a meat sack, skin sack, being blender, etc. Call it what you will—it serves as a physical being translator, transforming your being to adapt to any planetary conditions. This morph orb allows my Maresan vessel to cosmetically alter and adapt to long durations within Arth's atmosphere. As I touch the orb, I feel its attraction toward me. Ariyan suggests, "It's best to swallow it once it's warmed." I nestle the slippery, slick, icy surface next to my warm chest. Its diameter is the width of my mid-section. As I try to refrain from fearing this to be a choking hazard, my curiosity resurfaces, and I telepathically pry, *"Apollo, why go through the trouble of coaxing me into my resting unit, if you knew I was permitted to travel with you all?"*

Apollo looks at Cassiopeia and Ariyan, and replies sheepishly, "I wanted to continue one of my favorite rituals. I just love telling the story of Sir Reginald."

Feeling warm, and no sense of fear, I swallow the orb and quickly retort, *"Well, do you know it's my favorite story too?"*

Apollo looks at me, lifting his chin up, then back down to meet my gaze, "How can that be, if it's my favorite story?" It was our turn to engage in a moment of playfulness.

The moment passes, and Cassiopeia chimes in, "Mine too—and I'm just in time for my favorite part!" She stands up and turns around to look at the three of us. "This is where the star-crossed lovers communicate." As she begins, I can feel my most powerful tentacles pull together into a pair of legs. My physical shift gives me bliss I've never felt. Cassiopeia focuses on me as it's taking place. She leans in and lightly squeezes my left knee under the covers before continuing, "Reginald had never experienced engagement with a complementary prana source, but what he was feeling needed no explanation."

Cassiopeia now gets down on her knees in front of Ariyan and me, "From the moment she entered Reginald's awareness, she knew she could and wanted to spend all eternity with this radiant bringer of light. They both felt it; and maybe in another lifetime, they were together, but not this one. Here, they were strangers passing by in space. Fate still connected them to one moment on a path, but traveling in different directions. To have balance in all realities, this was one where their lights were not destined for one another. He knew this too, even though he yearned to redirect his divinity for even . . . even one moment longer in the passing of *his* belaved starlight."

Cassiopeia then shifted her eyes to Apollo, "And, oh—you best believe Andromeda knew his intentions. Reginald had just taken notice of her, whereas Andromeda knew of his existence long before he achieved motion. He failed to see her, but make no mistake, she saw him before his wonderful journey even began. She wished to be with Reginald when he was light-years away, but in discovering herself, she knew that those around him were always going to want him to show them the way. She could see it in his wake fallen particles from his Self, clinging to his radiance, wanting him to shine big and bright while they coasted along, following blindly with no intended direction. He was still holding on to too much for too many, and it was not being reciprocated. He needed someone who was willing to do for him what he was doing for everyone else. And she was willing to be that someone. Like her, he was being called by a desire to explore beyond—not outer spaces, but innermost places. It was not finding home; it was feeling at home."

Cassiopeia softened her voice, "That is when she fell in lave with Reginald and wanted him to be free; because when you are in lave, you only desire for others to know unconditional lave and happiness." At this point, I can't tell if it's my morphing two arms or the peaking part of the story; but an overwhelming sensation course through my body, wanting to grab both of my duality guardians and hold them close together.

Apollo jumps in, "Reginald knew not of this before proclaiming . . ." Apollo turns to Cassiopeia, who does not return his longing gaze—but instead purses her lips, concealing a coy smile while listening to his words, "'. . . Of all my moments, I choose to stay in this one forever.'"

Cassiopeia replies, as if she was the starlight, "Not wishing to be the restraint or downfall of this determined star who was a destined legend by all those who followed, or would soon be blessed by the wakening he would bring forth, Andromeda proclaimed, 'I mark you free from ever being deterred by another, by bestowing unto you an expression of unconditional bliss: To lave is to live. To live is to flow. To flow is to give. To give is to grow. In all of our moments, this we must know. Abracadabra.'" I look back and forth between my duality guardians, wondering if either of them would stray from their paths to be together.

Cassiopeia clears her throat, "Right after this message was communicated, Andromeda sped up, avoiding any possible collision with Reginald. Intentionally, a small bright fragment was left in his path, as she continued on without looking back. What she did next was not known to be possible. Lady Andromeda relinquished her strong nuclear force and shed all of her beautiful luster in a marvelous display that cannot be recreated. For those who didn't match her speed, it appeared to be an erratic explosion—POOF! For Reginald, relatively matching her speed, she gracefully dwindled down to nothing, in a long stream of stardust—a fiery, flickering dance. She intentionally led a solo choreographed dance, swaying with her lively hum, and then she flashed out of existence and brought complete silence."

Apollo now joins Cassiopeia on the floor; his right hip nestled by her left thigh. He leans over to kiss Cassiopeia's exposed shoulder, before picking up the story, "Reginald would have halted right there in his tracks if he hadn't been soaring forward to collect the last glint of glister left by his belaved. The moment she had left her speck for him, compared to the moment he collected it, now felt like lifetimes apart. Sir Reginald was filled with a feeling of obsession, followed by depression, which then grew to protection and now spiraled into deprivation. Reginald connected with the speck, and—"

Ariyan throws his arms up. "BOOM! Half of Sir Reginald called it quits at the mark of their intersection where his belaved zoomed by, hurling the other half Reginald forward with his belaved speck tucked away. Phased, but still determined, Reginald

58

continued to go forth into the darkness—cloaked in a great loss, he was unsure of his true direction."

Apollo picks it back up. "Those who were traveling in his wake began to falter and drop off, and past parts of him turned back, longing to stay with the other, more seemingly grounded half. It appeared that Sir Reginald was fading out to others within this space of nothingness."

Ariyan shifts his body to create a 90-degree swivel between me and Apollo. "That's what he wanted to do, but it was not what divinity intended for this reality. See, Andromeda's small speck left behind was destined to follow his course and grow with him! This was unknown to Reginald until he began to settle in and slow down. Only then did he realize that this speck was determined to continue forward, regardless of him stopping. No, it was not about to slow down. In fact, because of its size, not bulky and massive like Reginald, it was much quicker, and picking up speed!"

Ariyan focuses on me. "Reginald tried to restrain the speck, but realized it was going to get away from him. He knew if he didn't speed up by shedding his bulky mass, he would lose his little speck forever. He was not willing to risk that by carrying his burden of unnecessary matter." Ariyan makes fists in front of his face, and continues, "Inspired by this tiny speck who was 100-percent committed to finding its spot in this universe, in that moment of discovery, Reginald realized that in order for him to grow that committed in his intention, he was going to need to let go of everything that did not align with his will to get home. He aspired to be as committed to his journey as this speck of glister; no longer was he going to be the reason as to why he was not already there."

I feel as if I'm hearing this story for the first time as all the tiny hairs on my body rise. Is this sensation excitement or anxiety? I do not wish to interrupt Ariyan to ask—this is my favorite part of this tale! I glance over at Cassiopeia, who requites my attention. She reaches up and covers my arm with her delicate hand; she instantly feels my raised hairs. She winks at me, strokes my arm hairs down, and returns her attention to Ariyan. I follow suit. Ariyan hasn't even noticed our silent exchange. He continues, "As soon as Reginald was willing to let go, he experienced no pain in shedding layers, as he had had to do earlier when colliding into other cosmic entities. This time, when shedding himself, he felt liberated. It seemed effortless to remove his baggage. For those who do not understand the experience of letting go—from the outside looking in—it can appear self-destructive. Those who fear such unknown liberation default by turning away; in doing so, they neglect full comprehension of letting go by choosing the consolation of fearing flow."

Apollo clears his throat. "Reginald now understood why his lave did not stay, as he glances at his enormous other half, refusing to continue beyond the intersection. To remain in that moment would mean he would have to hold on to the past and return to being stagnant. Blissfully moving forward, Reginald dwindles down to a small speck. Just like Andromeda's speck, he too desired to be 100 percent committed to finding his true place calling to his innermost self. He was no longer responsible for those who blindly followed. They did not wish to understand where he was going, so they wouldn't understand what it took to get there. He didn't understand what his lave was doing while he thought he watched her disappear, but now he did. He most certainly remembered what it was like when he watched her dwindle away, but fate now granted him the duality to experience both sides of self-discovery. With intent, she simply let go of everything that no longer served her. Looking back to those following him, he realized that not all would understand at this moment what he was about to do either; and that was okay. His experience would be understood by those who truly were ready to shed what no longer served them, in hopes to move forward and live their most radiant lives."

As Apollo drapes his arm around Cassiopeia and rests his head on her shoulder, he confidently states, "Looking unto them, he was thankful to be on this side of self-discovery, just like his belaved—no longer wishing for happiness, but pursuing it 100 percent! For those in his wake who truly desired to pursue their own truths in happiness, he gave them the courage to go beyond their fearful states and find it. For those who desire to find it, it cannot be done without first recognizing this to be true—you must overcome the fear of the unknown. You have to make that choice to overcome this fear, before you can ever move forward; and only when you are ready . . . Well, regardless of others' readiness, Reginald's time of discovery was upon him."

With her corner-mouth, coy smile, Cassiopeia shifts gears. "Sir Reginald gained speed as he lost more and more clouds of glister, and as he dwindled down, so did the streaming left behind in his wake. He was now almost down to the size of his belaved speck and matching her speed. He dwindled down until he could hear his lave's hum on a much higher frequency. It remained within this speck, 'In every way I get a little bit better; in every way I grow a little bit more! You might say you wanna stay here forever, but it is worth it to let go 'n explore!' The melody repeated three more times, as Reginald became the same size as his belaved speck. He joined in their first duet. The binary beats continued out." Ariyan starts humming out of tune, which ensues laughter.

This is my favorite part of the story—Apollo, Cassiopeia, and Ariyan raise up their hands in tight little balls and leaning in, bring them close to me. I look at their hands—for the first time, I can join in with my two fists. Such a surreal sensation, my fingernails touching my palms. I bring two fists next to theirs. Ariyan chin-nods towards me to finish the story. I say it slowly, "On the cusp of being seen as notting, Egginald became eve'yting in a b'illiantly 'adiant... f'ash!" Instantly, we open our hands and wave our fingers in sync. I will master speaking.

Cassiopeia reaches over and begins tickling me! The sensation is unimaginable, the sensitivity of her connection is so impactful, and I urgently feel like my hueman form is going to burst at the seams! That doesn't happen. I stay contained, and the only thing that bursts out is laughter. There is no fear—quite the opposite, in fact, because every bit of my body is trembling with lave, and there are no screams of horror, only gasps of joy and bliss to be had. The tickling turns into a shower of kisses, and the warmest hugs. I sit up, and now move the long dark-brown curls out of my face. Oh, what delight this hueman experience is! Oh! What wonders await me in this reality, with my clan, my life, my light? I lave this feeling of uncertainty. Perhaps other celestial beings don't know how to lave each moment, even at times that don't seem all that radiant. Being born into my clan, I was destined to know lave like this; what a divine match. None else like it. Apollo concludes, "And as the story goes, the glistery trail left behind by Sir Reginald is the Reginald galaxy, and the stream left behind by Lady Andromeda is the Andromeda galaxy." Ariyan inserts, "Oh! Oh! And the point that marks the intersection is in the center where the Sun is located." I nod my head along with Ariyan.

I look back at my guardians just as they start fading away. I look at Ariyan, who's fading as well. I panic. As I try to stand up and grab them, I stumble and it goes dark. Where did my lave go? *SNAP*.

4 MY INSIGHTFUL THOUGHTS

FLASH. The end of my beloved memory; for now, I suppose. I'm curious why it raced back to me, so vividly. It did give me the certainty to move forward, but those pixelated beings said I would only recollect on the incomplete occurrence, so I shouldn't have memories that are already complete.

I look all around, hoping to see the five of them. Why was I able to draw on that memory so clearly? Was there something I was missing? I let it go, but not soon enough. I hear that inner voice, **_"What was not complete?"_** Still in darkness, I scream out in frustration, "I don't know!"

Soprano assures me in a low tone, *"Sure you do. Perhaps you just need to think of a valid question to what you don't remember, and—"*

Now I'm angry. *SNAP*. I cut them off, "Perhaps you don't remember that you were going to let me be."

Baritone clarifies, *"Not in moments like this. We understand the desire to be stubborn, but—"*

I lose it, "I am not stubborn! I was brought back here with no memory—and the two that I've gotten you try to invade and dissect, like . . . like . . ."

Bass slides in, *"We are simply assisting you in understanding why certain memories might be revisited and what might complete them. Worry not. We cannot see your memories unless you allow us to explore with you. Please trust that we want nothing more than for you to join us in our mission to—"*

I go ballistic! *SNAP*. "I knew you were trying to use me! I will never join your mission!" *SNAP*. "Never! And how can I trust that you really cannot see my memories? You could just be lying!" *SNAP*. "Liars!" *SNAP*. "Liars!" *SNAP*. "Lying liars!" *SNAP*. *SNAP*.

I'm exhausted. A great deal of silence goes by, before anything is said. Caught in a stalemate, I grow lonely, but they say nothing, so I ask, "Are you still . . . here?" Nothing. Still engulfed by darkness, not ready to go into the light, I reach out to them through the inter-com, "*Are you still there?*" I hope to hear them; I really hope they did not leave me. I'm sorry. *CLICK*. I hope they can hear me. *CLICK*.

"Always." *CLICK*. I don't know who inter-commed me. It sounds like Soprano, mixed with Bass and Baritone. Could it be all of them at once? *CLICK*. "*It's all relative to openness, Sonder. Communication on the inter-com level only works with beings operating on higher frequency connections. When you detach and go into a lower level of consciousness, you will not be able to communicate with us. We will be able to hear you, just not the other way around. Just keep in mind how*

many thoughts of yours are" *CLICK* *"ascending, versus* *SNAP* *descending."*

Baritone sets me at ease through telepathy, *"Now, about your memories. You live within a realm where memories are like skin suits you enter. Similar to a skin suit, you cannot enter a vessel—until given permission by its being. Consent is necessary, and we are clear you have not given consent."* *CLICK*. This makes sense. I feel a bit silly. I know they are not liars, and they're trying to help.

I acknowledge them telepathically, *"Thank you for your guidance. I am discovering how . . . stubborn I still am. I haven't a clue as to why I revisited both of those memories."*

Bass encourages me, *"Understandable. As you go through more and more memories, be mindful of how you feel now. We hadn't even entered your memories, and you became hostile. Now imagine how touchy sleepers get when we want to vessel project on them."* I haven't a clue what vessel projection is, but I'm okay without having it happen to me. I let them know, *"I will keep this in mind, and stick to what I know, which is resolving my curiosities by asking questions."*

Just then my inner voice returns, ***"What qualified me for my skin suit?"*** My mind is racing for a truth. Why is that the question? Letting go of my skepticism, I focus on answering the question. Perhaps there was something incomplete about that memory I overlooked. I was thinking why that story time remained out of all the times I heard that story, and maybe it was because I was given my skin suit.

CLICK. Thinking back on that trip to Arth, that was the last time my clan was together to share that story.

CLICK. I've been on Arth since then. It was never discussed, but we never went back after our assignment in Minnesota. I did not know at that time, but now my curiosity drifts to a depressing possibility. Did my guardians know that the four of us wouldn't be going back? Along with keeping my morph orb a secret, did they keep that a secret as well? No response. I don't know if the pixelated beings know the answer to this question, but it now drives my direction.

My guardians lave me, so what in the universe would try to drive us apart? The more I become connected with this curiosity, the more the light from the passageway draws me in. I hover cautiously right on the brim. The last sense of safety hangs within the threshold of the corridor. I smile and ask myself what is safe anymore. *CLICK*. All at once, I shift out of the cusp, and into an abrupt, over-exposed light that is so piercing that I wince; a surge of pain through my—oh! An absence of pain—yet, I feel, I know this to cause pain. Strange. I have memories of how things feel, but no physical consequences.

I must have damaged my senses or destroyed them. Momentarily, I feel incapable of sight. Then, little by little, different gradient hues trickle into my awareness. Oh, radiant prisms of color! I see images racing around in hot pink, blood orange, chartreuse, and cobalt—Huzzah! The more I take in, the more the blurred shapes become defined, rigid bodies, all zipping around in nauseating little figure-eights and circular patterns. Like clogs and cogs in an ancient timekeeper. Their actions are so loud I barely notice the audible repetition of the same phrase: "Oh my, oh my." I think of this and wish to stop watching these monotonous faces in time.

A deafening roar vibrates the walls. Frantic barks and shouts, all forms of panic vociferate down from the upper-levels. I glide forward and see two floors above me, with hysterical spacers doing the same runaround as they were doing on this level; tick-tock, tick-tock echoes in my head. I hold guilt for having caused this. I blankly stare to the center of this hall of collected chaos, and see a giant Arthling eerily staring me down. He seems disturbingly calm in a sea of frantic Maresans. Why is a hueman on a Maresan ship? As he stares right at me, I see him—it—glitch. It's a hologram? I glide just a bit to the left, and its focus seems to be locked onto me.

This hologram begins to speak: "When experiencing chaos, stay curious, and stay connected." I do not think this message is effective. The chaos ensues, because they think I'm dead.

Screams range from blame to guilt: "Why did she kill herself?" "Was there anything they could have done?" "Why did they let it happen?" "She was always different." "She just wanted attention." "Why wasn't I nicer to her?"

I scream out, "I'm alive! I'm here! That video lied!" The chaos ensues. I must show them. I go to the first prana being I can reach. I try to stop her, but she pushes past, and I'm avoided. I reach out for another prana, and then another. No acknowledgment; instinctively they redirect themselves around me. I am puzzled. After the sixth foolish attempt, I stand there, teleing, "*Can anyone see me? Do I still exist? What am I doing here? Where can I go to be heard?*"

My inner thoughts collect doubt, and I get caught up in an unwanted sensation. My lack of clarity and my existential cycle ensues. I stand here intently, waiting for my inner thoughts to form a concrete idea. There is no way for me to talk to them. They are operating at too low of levels, and aren't able to connect with my frequency. I can relate . . . I played their role not too long ago. *SNAP*. I think about Baritone spinning around in their nauseating circles—perhaps they had tried to stop this, and their results were the same as mine . . . How wicked I must have sounded to assume that the other pixelated beings were just mocking these distraught spacers; accusing them of not trying. How can you help when you cannot be seen? Looking at all these spacers run around in nauseating circles . . . Who am I to judge anyone? No! I will not beat myself up over this. I was ignorant, and will not blame or judge anyone for the actions they take in their own lives. As for me, I will continue forth in hopes of returning to my mission. Now, what is my next move? Suddenly I feel a sense of direction coming from inside, **_"We could head back into our dormitory. That seems practical."_**

That's a good idea, maybe we—oh! Wait . . . We? *CLICK*. Am I operating as two? No response. I begin looking around. Finally, I gaze up beyond eye level and marvel at the ceiling, which is jam-packed with many large screens. These screens are playing out multiple different images taking place in a desert-like setting; multiple different scenes and activities. Fire, tears, and ash. Lots of ash. I cannot get a clear sense of what is taking place, although I can get a sense that these are clips being replayed. Still images caught in time. Then I see him. Ariyan. Seeming to be completely still and alone. *SNAP*. I let you down, Yan.

My world goes silent. All I hear is the muffled words, "When experiencing chaos, stay curious, and stay connected." I feel lost looking at him; he appears to stand on top of the world. Still, center stage, on top of a suspended cage several meters off the ground. He wears a face of defeat, but not reacting like those I am surrounded by; I sense his silent anguish. The screen switches and I break away my gaze. I look inward. In the moment of looking in, I tele, *"How am I going to find myself?"* In an instant, the room begins to dim. The vibrant colors become dark silhouettes. Everything seems to slow down, and I now begin to beam an electric green aura. I lift up my appendages to my face. *CLICK*. Now I pulsate a red aura. Regardless of why I am glowing, my level of surprise is saturated and I barely respond to this. I am sure I will find out soon what triggered this action. I now tele, *"Which way should I go?"* Almost instantly, as if I summoned an escort, large red orbs materialize and glow, just to the left of my being. They hover about half a meter off the ground.

I begin to follow the red orbs, first avoiding the prana beings at all cost, and now I hover directly over the orbs in a straight path. Everything around me seems to almost melt away as I pass through the central terminal. The line of orbs leads me down a spiral ramp about nine meters below the initial entrance to Central Terminal. The final few orbs stop in front of a darkened corridor. Just as quickly as the orbs appeared, they seem to vanish. *POOF*. As they vanish, the hallway remains dark, except for a stream of light coming from one single passageway, about halfway down on the right side of this dark corridor. The passageway reveals light cream floor tiles and an aqua door frame. I effortlessly float toward the doorway that floods the hall with light. It is the light that draws me, as I escape the world of darkness. I glide past its threshold but cease further movement once I spot four resting units placed in the middle of the space.

I look into the room, and it is evident that the prana beings living here have not returned for some time now. Nothing hangs on the walls, besides a curtain halfway drawn over the window. There are two large standing black boxes with combination lock pads. And to the right of me is a smaller doorway; that's about it. I focus back on the center of the room. The four identical units are squarely pushed together—all elevated with drawers below for storage. Two units are covered with pillows and a single blanket each. The other two units have one pillow each and are littered with blankets. Only one bed is made perfectly, while the others are not. I cannot help but be drawn to the most disheveled unit littered with blankets. It looks as though it has been yearning for my return.

This room was assigned to me—it's my dormitory. It calls for me to rest once more; it wishes to serve its purpose for just a bit longer. Perhaps I was led here to collect some of my most precious belongings. I glide backward. I have no real desire or wish to rest, nor to collect any of these items that I left behind. Without the memories that gave them value, they are just items; but one item demands I take hold of it. It calls from my disheveled unit. I feel a sensation growing and yearning—search here and find me. I am curious . . . Who is me?

I crouch over the resting unit and begin searching. Like opening up a present, I begin throwing blankets on the floor. I then move my single pillow. Huzzah! A green journal. Was this mine? I pick the journal up and I feel it whisper, "Yes." Hovering just to the side of my resting unit, before opening my journal, I notice three American words written on the spine: 'My Insightful Thoughts'—MIT? I like it.

The book is embossed with many different symbols and patterns. I see that the front cover is held shut by an elastic strap connected from its back. On this strap is a tiny metal shield with a triangle broken up into four smaller triangles. I grab the shield, pull it off to the side with the strap, and open the journal. Before I get to the pages, I see something written on the reverse side of the cover. It's a note, with no dates or indication of when it was written. I begin to read:

You are about to embark on a mission . . . in many, many words.
The mission is simply to live life. Life is simple.
There is only one thing you need to know.
Life is a game.

In this game, you can take any route . . .

I stop reading and turn the page to the first entry. This is the problem with books; they always begin with some strange epilogue. It's as if they want to be mysterious, or something. Why do authors do that? They should just start with the book. I glance over and read the first page, marked July 10th, 1991, and begin:

Salutations, MIT –

This will be my first entry as I begin to practice formulating thoughts into "timed sequences." Now that I have been permitted access to my hueman skin suit, I am required to demonstrate basic concepts and understanding of the hueman conditioning. This includes reading, writing, and speaking the "language of business."

Ariyan was explaining something about it to me in my lesson today, but it was hard to concentrate on one thing while so many other thoughts and emotions wash in and out of my head. Staying focused seems difficult with so much stimuli. I do hope this gets easier. Being hueman is just so exciting. The sensation of being a water-based being instead of a mineral-based being is a trip in and of itself! I wonder if my skin suit will change colors like Apollo and Ariyan's does, or if I get to keep this color like Cassiopeia.

With the concepts and lessons we went over today, I am not quite sure I will be ready by the time we enter Arth's atmosphere. Everyone believes in me, so the least I can do is believe in myself. With Cassiopeia and Apollo being called away, I'm so glad I have Ariyan. He has a way of really not giving up on me—so far.

MIT — ARIYAN'S LESSON

FLASH. I jump back into this conversation mid-sentence, which fazes me slightly. Ariyan continues, "Like Mares, Arth cycles through four planetary seasons, which constantly repeat its phase changes."

Okay, a crash course of similarities between Mares and Arth. Stay focused. I'll get used to this; I hope. Jumps into memories become easier; I hope. Knowing that my journal entry talked about being over-stimulated, now having to find my bearings, it seems that this experience might be overwhelming.

I was just reading words on an oatmeal-colored paper, and now I've projected myself into a vivid collection of images. I cannot help that my eyes absorb all the spectrums of light filtering in and out of my viewpoint. I'm so glad to be back . . . Wait, what is Ariyan talking about?

I tune back in, "It is unknown when Arthlings started believing the planetary cycles determined their own life-advancing cycles. One Arth year for the planet does not equate to one allevelation for Arthlings; that is far too limiting for some . . . **and far too generous for most."**

Ariyan jokes, "Regardless of hueman beings' beliefs in their allevelation, it is important that you do not combine your cycle levels with the natural cycles of Arth. You might have multiple allevelations by the time Arth completes one full rotation. Each Arth cycle takes approximately three-hundred, sixty-four and a quarter rotations. Which—"

I interrupt, "Null weight! Tats stupper fast! Zits haft watt Mars takes to compete."
Ariyan looks at me, fairly amused. "YES way. That is SUPER fast. And IT IS HALF of WHAT MARES takes to COMPLETE one cycle. Susun, I am more surprised you heard me with your lack of attention than your lack of pronunciation. Listening isn't just with your ears. On Arth, many will think you are not engaged and rude, if you do not give your attention to those speaking. I am in front of you, and you are constantly looking up and behind your back. It's a bit distracting, and some might say rude."

Ariyan's point is made as I discontinue looking at my feet, and instantly look up at him. He clearly wants the best for me. Discourteously, I return my attention to this nicely textured mat we are both sitting on. I choose to enjoy this sensation of experiencing my calf skimming over the little ridges.

You never notice sensation as a Maresan, but with this Arthling body, it heightens the state of enjoyment to a level that cannot be ignored; like the

76

plate of air as one walks into a room while crossing the threshold of a passageway should not be missed. Everything should be admired and appreciated. Ariyan appears quite perturbed. I apologize, "My apollies. I watted to see if the bops on the mat mooed as I mooed my feet over dem."

A little less amused, but without defeat, Ariyan responds, "I can work practical physics education in today's lesson, after we complete the history sub-section." He looks down at the mat. "And NO APOLOGIES. You are learning. Now my curiosity is piqued to see if the BUMPS on the mat MOVE."

I am already looking at Ariyan, when he returns his attention and empathizes, "I remember what it was like adjusting to the heightened sensitivity of this body. And trust me—"

I interrupt him again, "You do? But jour capital is defend than mine!"

Ariyan chuckled, genuinely. "Sonder, you are in for a treat when we get to Arth. YOUR CAPSULE, MY CAPSULE, EVERYONE'S' CAPSULE. They all look DIFFERENT on the outside. They have an array of different hair colors and skin suit tones. See, on Mares, we all are very similar besides our height and length, because we have a very homogenous planet-like atmosphere. There isn't much need for evolution to have different physical traits, because they are not needed for survival or nutrient absorption. On Arth, which is about ten times larger, there is a huge need for variety for their primitive prana to survive and thrive. Blonde and brunette hair is just as common as red and black. Brown eyes are sometimes as common as blue. And wait until you see other dad bods in comparison to yang's capsule!" This gets me excited. I've never seen another capsule with brown eyes like mine. Cassiopeia, Apollo, and Ariyan all have blue. And red hair? How fascinating. I lave how animated Ariyan gets when teaching me.

Ariyan holds up his hand and I touch mine to his. Feeling the atom-thick plate of separation between us, he shares, "Sonder, there's a lot for you to catch up on. Not just the knowledge, but also the experience of being hueman. I do not know who invented morph orbs, but I am glad they allow us to fully experience an Arth-Maresan transformation experience. The senses within this capsule are extraordinary when used to make a connection. My capsule experiences heightened sensitivity to light, sound, and impulses in comparison to my Maresan capsule." As we sit hand-to-hand, I've already mastered six levels of my development with Ariyan teaching me everything he knows.

It seems flawless from the outside, but I know it's been a challenge trying to educate me. I feel ashamed at my lack of focus. "Apollies, Yan. I am distracted, and—"

Ariyan cuts me off. "You don't need to APOLOGIZE. Everyone's astonished how quickly you're gaining these lessons; honestly, I'm ashamed that others say how good I am as a teacher for you when you're the one doing the work. To be honest, if you didn't ask so many questions, all I would be doing is feeding you outdated misinformation. Based on what I learned, nothing really changes, just the places and the faces. Racism is still a thing, because the targeted groups are shifted periodically. Pollution is still a thing, because industries are still allowed to produce using little to no sustainable resources without any repercussions. Oh—and equality is so misunderstood, they praise civil obedience over civil disobedience, because governing powers are still allowed to shame individual parties who question the broken links in their snagged system."

I can tell Ariyan wants to go off the set lesson plan, but he resists obediently wanting to lead by example. "As for distractions, they are common for the work we are doing on Arth. I find it best to observe, and then ask questions. However, you might find success in doing it your way. Luckily for us, huemans function strongest through spiritual connection, even though they might not be aware of it. So even if you do not know, you can usually feel it out."

I absorb what Ariyan is saying. "You can pick up on their feelings?"

Ariyan warns, "Yes, just try not to stare while tuning into them. Even if they want to connect, most Arthlings have forgotten what it's like to be seen, so too much direct eye contact makes them uncomfortable; especially if you're not talking. Even without eye contact, you can easily read them. Arthlings have forgotten that they are constantly communicating with their language of—"

I chime in, *"Telepathy!"*

Ariyan holds up one index finger and touches his nose. "That is a brilliant guess. My first choice as well! Most Arthlings operate in too low of frequencies; they are not capable of telepathy. Their primal language is of the body. Body language is constant, but the hueman conditioning tries to mask it with opposing verbal communication. Without communicating vocally, Arthlings would instinctively recognize an awful lot about themselves and others much quicker; but that makes them uncomfortable—so they avoid it by talking. They hide behind their world of words—oh! And add another layer of confusion called sarcasm. Think of vocal language as a smokescreen; and sarcasm as a brick wall. If you become proficient, it's easy to go undetected while interacting with huemans on our MAD missions."

CLICK. We want to blend in. I tele, *"Is that why our duality guardians tried to have me speak before communicating with me telepathically? Was it for safety?"*

Ariyan grows a bit stiff. "Yes. And my mistake has hindered you . . ." He looks down in such despair it almost frightens me. "I will never, ever dishonor our clan legacy, ever. I just, I just—wasn't aware I could hinder your learning abilities."

I lean in with much excitement. *"Ariyan, if it wasn't for you, I would not have been able to communicate at—"*

He cuts me off. "I was out of line. If you did not know you could communicate telepathically, you would be a fluent speaker right now—you would have been forced to speak if you wanted to communicate. Now I live with shame knowing I crippled the most beautiful butterfly forever."

I empathize with Ariyan; he did nothing wrong. I wish to remind him of this. He blames himself for connecting with me when I felt lost. He continues, "I swore to protect you, and all I've done is shamed our clan. I'm the reason everyone questions your advancements—they think I am giving you unfair advantages. Who could blame them? That's why I promise to . . . to . . ." I almost jump in, but realize how complicated it would be.

Ariyan looks up at me, with so much regret, "I promise to always do right by you. And I will make sure you are the most articulate Forkins in our clan using the"—Ariyan holds up his air quotes before finishing—"business language."

I think for a second, just listen to his feelings. How much pain did I cause him? I wish to reach out to him, but how would I explain that I'd jumped back to my birth—and into this memory for that matter?

Saying anything could make things more complicated. What could I say that could make it less complicated? I tele, *"Curious, why is American called the business language?"*

"Insightful question," Ariyan assures. *CLICK*. "There are so many languages, but hueman beings— a majority now associate the worldwide business language as English, although you are correct, it should be called American at this point. So many alterations to definitions and spellings . . . 'colonel' and 'subtly' are two of my favorite words to see spelled."

Ariyan looks as though he is enjoying an inside joke until I inquire, *"If spoken language is unclear, why not just re-establish body language? Especially when the majority of the world did not grow up with American as their native tongue? I mean, I might be biased, but I'd rather learn body language than keep practicing American too."*

"Well . . ." Ariyan seems almost lost, and then all at once returns, "The Universal Nation wants to teach them *the* universal language. We are here as a MAD unit, trying to teach lave. It's taking a while though, because they seem to like having miscommunication in their language. This could be a whole lesson in and of itself; I really do not know if we have time—"

I interrupt him telepathically, *"But I do not understand why we're trying to teach them the universal language of lave if they do not comprehend it. Why not go back, remind them of body language, and have them revert. Why add layers, when we can remove them? I mean, do they have anything even close to lave on their planet? And why is this business language group so powerful, especially if it's only the businesses that get advantages? Who made that game up?"*

Ariyan pauses. I can sense frustration. Then he speaks in an exaggerated way. "Sonder, in order to have change, you need to go with the flow, before starting your own course. If we want to help, we must first understand the way of their reality. The Arth prana created it, and the hueman conditioning embodies it. The world functions for business, it's the flow of their society—fueled by a value called money. Money, which the majority of the huemans do not have. And the little that they do have, they hold on desperately, then become attached to gaining more of it. It's idiotic how valuable money has become."

Ariyan raises an eyebrow for emphasis, "For enough money, you can buy living celestial beings—literally living prana!" I'm shocked, but also shamelessly curious. Ariyan can clearly tell this by his reaction. "I'm not making this up! I know what you are thinking—it's moronic! I mean, finding equality within their own race is hard enough, but try convincing them that their newborn matters just as much as a village pig, which is just as valuable as their ex-partner. Sure, the importance is relative to the individual, but we cannot seem to get them past the basics. They remain stagnant, and do not listen?"

I ask him, "How dud they newt listen? Can they newt fill the pain they cost?"

Ariyan does not even look at me. "They DO NOT listen, because they are too righteous—too entitled. They DO NOT FEEL the pain they CAUSE, because they are so disconnected." He looks up at me, "They feel justified in taking without questioning if they are to gain. They justify what was sacrificed for their satisfaction—regardless of another prana being's loss; no questions asked. And it's not entirely the hueman's fault that most never ask questions. They've been brainwarshed to fear questioning and the risk of being marked ignorant. They have been desensitized to see, feel, or question the pain they inflict."

Ariyan holds my hands. "Arth children seem to remember ignorance is bliss. They are never fearful to ask all their questions. Even when they are not given answers, they will keep throwing their questions out there. Unfortunately, only a few of the billions of children asked enough questions and discovered they had a choice to never grow up. So you can't blame those who quit playing."

Ariyan takes a breath and proceeds, "Yes. Playing; it's a huge part of life. Perhaps that's why they call it *perpetual catch* 22. Asking questions is the way to get out of the looping circumstance if you get caught in it. Ironically, most huemans get cheated out of learning to ask questions as being fun. The fun comes from understanding it's a game of catch. Sadly, huemans have become fearful of catching new ideas thrown to them; as if they will be thought foolish for not getting them right away. But you only learn by catching what is thrown at you. Maybe teachers have a disdain for catching, and only like throwing. I can honestly say I've been experiencing that as I am teaching you. When I am busy throwing ideas to you, I get caught off-guard when you throw something back at me. I should expect it though, because in learning—there are always questions sporadically popping up. It feels wonderful to teach and throw, but I should embrace not knowing that I might learn and catch something from you, as my pupil. I have grown fearful of looking foolish if I cannot answer some of your questions correctly, so I lash out when you give me new ideas. Funny, conditioning has me in this endless game of just wanting to teach, a perpetual game of catch, and yet I only like to throw to you. I wonder where my stigma of getting your new ideas comes from."

I tilt my head as Ariyan continues, "Being exposed to Maresan customs granted us the awareness to know we can create and relate with anything instantaneously. Like Arthlings, we are still practicing and learning to find balance in our Self, but now we will be surrounded by a population that has forgotten this is just a game. Regardless, if it seems harder when surrounded by hypocrites, who lack the will to find their balance, it really is all the same."

I ask, "What's a hypocrite?"

Ariyan explains, "Hypocrites are individuals who say they dislike something that they themselves do." Ariyan returns eye contact, "Which is why the phrase is so taboo. Hypocrites create their hypocrisy, often talking about how much they do not like something—and then they do it!"

I inquire, "Why, exactly?"

Ariyan grins, "Because Arthlings have been choosing hypocrisy over responsibility since the beginning! They know of balance, and yet they focus heavily on the changing variables, not constants. The state of being hueman comes from finding balance in their living trinity: mental, physical, and spiritual. The spiritual state, which goes on forever. The physical state, which is limited and very fragile. And the mental state, which acts as the linchpin connecting the limited to the limitless to the present state. Often, huemans choose to examine and explore their physical self to a fault, and if examined too far without connecting to the spiritual state, it could limit their self-lave. By decreasing selflessness, they increase selfishness, perpetuating self-love. It perturbs

85

me how much love they truly feel for themselves and others . . . like they don't think they are worth being laved." I wonder if only Arthlings demonstrate this state of hypocrisy.

Ariyan looks listless, "For those who do not practice this, they often will repeat the same levels over and over again without being aware. Like the eighty-year-old made millionaire who still has"—air quote—"'daddy issues'. It's a perfect example of winning the game of business, while losing the game of life. Or households speaking out against slavery and human trafficking, but see no problem in having household pets and eating animmel products. A perfect example of fighting for prana equality, while fueling the inequality of prana . . . It's been a long period of hypocrisy for huemans who lack responsibility in areas of life that they judge themselves so harshly in. They talk up massive smoke screens—not wanting to see their own fears festering from within."

Ariyan pontificates, "That's why we must be willing to practice what they might not understand: equality. When equality is practiced, prana realizes that all cycles are equal. For me, my first level of determination is just as important as my last one of acknowledgment. For you, your first level of awareness is just as important as oneness. No level is greater or more valuable; we master our levels in no particular order. However, sleepers on Arth do not talk about levels as we do; and they have a specific order they must master before transcending. They have it much easier, but they make it difficult. From level one of security up to level twelve of commitment, since most are unaware of the game, they play with a huge disadvantage."

Ariyan rationalizes, "Again it's not entirely their fault. Based on their understanding passed down in hueman conditioning, most Arthlings are born and raised with meek concepts of lave covered in personal fears of the unknown. Arthlings are raised by those who have come before them, who were also brought up the same way. Fear grows in the community and anyone from outside their community is ostracized, or worse . . ." Ariyan motions with a hand around his neck. I comprehend his indication of death as he continues. "It's wild to think racism evolves more rapidly than acceptance, and revenge quicker than forgiveness. Every generation has it—but they never think it is as bad as the generation that came before them: crusading for religions, burning the witches, gassing the jews, lynching the negros, smearing the queers, terrorizing the Muslims, cleansing the transgenders, overthrowing government cults, and the recent technophobia tirades."

I blink furiously, "And they aways look ootwars at groots that's different?"

Ariyan chuckles, "Yes, they ALWAYS look OUTWARDS at GROUPS that ARE different. The fascinating truth is it temporarily numbs the inner fears they struggle with by blaming something else for their feelings of discomfort or frustration. By Allah, instead of resolving their obstacles, lower-level prana beings like handling their struggles by trying to destroy it; but as we know—"

87

I cut in, "No prana can be created, or destroyed, just mood."

Ariyan cringes, "Just MOVED. That is correct." His delightful demeanor returns, "They don't want to move, or grow, because fear creates a delusion in stardust that if things stop moving around them, then life will be simple life; and that's considered success."

I ask telepathically, *Why would they want that? Don't they know about Sir Reginald?"*

Ariyan rolls his eyes. "Well, for starters, we know that not all of Reginald's stardust kept moving. Some prana still believe staying stagnant is the superior plan; moving is too maniac. Also, for anyone who works hard in their labyrinth of life—Arthling or not—hitting a wall is never easy to admit. So for settlers who feel they have come so far, the last thing they want to be told is to reconsider their current direction."

Ariyan sighs heavily, "Most prana then become stagnant, adding to the superiority complexed driven being." He backs up a bit. "Again, in a universe built on equality, balance is a constant practice as we grow. This is why we would do well to remember, even if you never do it, we always have the option of turning around and going back. Never stay stuck; keep moving. This always seems to be missed when hitting a wall. You, for example . . . It's hard to get the pronunciation of American language down, so you keep reverting back to using telepathy. You speak eloquently when confident, yet you are sloppy with tongue placement when speaking, so you avoid practicing when rushing."

Like a cold hand tracing down my back, discomfort is triggered when a weakness is exposed. Ariyan knows I'm triggered, as he continues, "I do not say that to discourage you—American is one of the hardest languages to learn. Their phonetics are inconsistent and seem random; certain definitions for words have been rewritten so many times it's comical. Like bad means 'bad', but also 'good'. We have to be willing to master American to appease Arthlings and not blow our covers."

Everything Ariyan shares rings true. His passion picks up, "Shoot, it's crazy how much we cater to them—they are just as alien as we are. Maresans are no different than Arthlings; aside from the respect we show other prana beings. Some Arthlings would shoot another Arthling just for being born in a different shade of meat bag. Almost all of them would shoot us because we were born on a different space rock. Regardless of what they would do, I will always help them, because I know they are someone's loved one. Sometimes I wish to be as close-minded, but what would I accomplish? I feel like they just pretend to forget we're all floating in space, made up of stardust, and they still justify shooting us. I just wish that once we'd open fire just to—"

I jerk back and place both my hands at my sides. His face quickly changes, once he sees how I react. He requests, "Do not take what I say as gospel. I am still grasping what this all means to me. My experiences paint a very doomed outlook for Arth. That is not the truth . . . if it was, we would not be assigned all these missions trying to rehabilitate the sleepers. But the more I see, the more I have to suppress this emotional disgust. They desire to elevate, but will *never* escape their own states of being, because they enjoy wallowing in their distracted cycles of self-deprivation and depression. They choose their perpetual catch twenty-two in life: praise the victor, and play the victim; and never connect that they are one in the same, so they perpetuate their villainous vices."

I can hear an unmistakable sadness in his voice. "It's bittersweet, the hueman conditioning. A capsule of internal enslavement. They can only impose it on others, because they already entrapped their spirit while shackling their minds in mental cages. The mind is cruel and plays tricks on them. They are brainwarshed to believe chains are only made of metal." He chuckles, "Money is the most powerful form of shackle." He holds up an open hand to emphasize, "A perfect utopian sphere inhabited by leeches that create their own problems—pretending all their drama is happening to them, and not through them."

Ariyan quickly makes his open hand into a fist. "The leech-like, sucking lifeforms on their imprisoned planet, living lifetime sentences for all eternity . . . until they completely use up their planet. They deserve the world they end up with."

Ariyan looks very menacing now. What emotions is he drawing from? Never have I heard these words from him. Ariyan—someone who I thought only knew how to elevate and bring light into any and all situations. He's talking as if the whole hueman race was a self-destructive beast. I wish to remind him of the duality within all prana beings. What if their time on Arth isn't just for them?

CLICK. Yeah! What if it's for us to master responding and assisting others? I almost interject until I become aware of his furrowed brow. Naively, I ask, "Wad art you luking at?"

Ariyan immediately returns to a stoic composure, "Two things: Susun—I am beginning to grow a slight irritation toward you; it's no fault of yours. Forgive me for these thoughts. They seem automatic. I never noticed them. Usually, while you're in deep REM during these stages, and I'm given all the attention of our guardian; my role is now reversed in this educational platform. It's frustrating not knowing all the answers to your questions."

Ariyan seems to think it over, "I don't know everything, and I never asked most of your questions. I am worried that I do not have nearly enough wisdom or experience to cover even the basics."

Ariyan collects his thoughts, "Second, little sister—truth has many points of view, and even though I am aware of it, I cannot seem to expand myself beyond my own biased opinions. As I think back to how I was taught, most of my exposure saw equal lightness and darkness." He reminisces, "My education provided insight. I feel as though I only give darkness. Like a two-dimensional being trying to point out a three-dimensional shape. I am trying, but my attempts in my teaching land flat. You are going to have to manifest a lot of lightness to gain clarity on my shadows. Please forgive me. Truly, my intention is to succeed in providing you a glowing education. I am not as effective as my leaders, Apollo and Cassiopeia—errr"—Ariyan makes the air quotes again—"Mom and Dad."

As much as he uses them, I still do not know when it is appropriate to use the air quotes. Just like sarcasm, I will honor it, but never use it.

I see a new sadness in Ariyan. "I miss them, but they will return soon. Very soon."

I place my hand back up, indicating to go hand-to-hand. He looks at it, and then back at me. I say slowly, determined to say it correctly, "Then do not see me as a pupil any longer. I am now your peer." He places his hand to mirror mine, takes a breath, and nods in acceptance.

FLASH. We went on as peers—partners in pursuing information. I am flooded with many images of us, continuously learning alongside one another. Even though our universes had different experiences, we often shared the same points of view.

FLASH. I regain focus on a very similar scene, both of us wearing slightly different outfits. During this lesson together, we discussed where on Arth most prana were waking, and how likely they were to stay woke.

Ariyan concludes, "That's why the Universal Nation created opportunities for *data collecting*, like we do on our MAD clan unit missions. That's why I wanted to become a spacer. I desire to learn how to make a difference for prana on my own. I have no idea what Spacer University is like, but I'm excited! We are all stardust, and we do not belong to any one world. Sometimes, I even forget that. I get stuck in Maresans and Arthlings—but what about Fenuis, or Guupiter . . . It's crazy how often I forget that Apollo is from another galaxy. There is so much to expand on. We might be proud of where our physical matter comes from, but in the end, each galaxy is made up of the same lights and lumps; I just hope I don't become pretentious after learning more about it."

Ariyan's voice became softer. "With success in the space program, we will awaken enough hueman beings to reboot this planet into reviving, self-sustaining practices. If we could successfully have the mass population be woke rather than sleeping, this would be a whole new game. It's fascinating—and extremely stimulating!" He appears to think back to what he said before. "Hmmm . . . it's moments like this that rekindle my hope for Arthlings—you know, to not be damned to self-destruction." He smiles. "That ability to—"

I burst in, "To create a massive waking for sleepers on Arth." *CLICK*. That's what I did!

Ariyan beams, "Accurate, Susun. I might be saying too much about this, but that's why the UN created Spacer University. The program's intention is to train us in how to help Arthlings align with their true intentions."

Ariyan seems to glow, "That is why I vow to be of service for the curious ones around their world. I will discover when opportunities are present when their minds are open and willing to connect. Through my training, I will understand what is acceptable to shine enlightenment on when a mind is open. There is an infinite array of possibilities; I'm sure it will be more magical than I can possibly imagine." *CLICK*. That's what I will figure out again.

Ariyan continues, "I was not very open before when you used to ask me your very thought-provoking questions. I was a very naive teacher, and was not willing to catch the questions you threw to me when I did not have answers. Since you've had me alter my educational style, I feel more empowered when you ask me questions that I do not yet have a response to. I am a bit ashamed of who I was. Do you forgive the mentor I used to be?"

I nod, and request, "As long as you can do the same for the distracted pupil I used to be!"

He nods, but says, "No promises."

We both laugh and complete the lesson with a laving hug. The sensation of sibling lave lingers, as he slowly begins to fade away; so does the rest of the memory, but not my commitment to rediscovering how to create a massive wake.

5 COMMANDER'S VISIT

FLASH. I am hovering next to my resting unit. I feel a bit drained. Slowly, I lower myself down into the comfort of the unit. The comradery with Ariyan drifts away. How long was I in that memory? I look around and feel another memory hovering over me. My inner intelligence encourages me, **_"Go now."_**

Without hesitation, I allow the memory to come to me. I choose to get comfortable for this one, not knowing how long it will be. Lying down, I focus on everything and nothing. Little by little, the room starts shifting, as do the colors . . . and the temperature?

FLASH. Now lying in the center of a room on a circular rug, I watch a ceiling fan mock me in the scorching afternoon heat. It continues to rotate in a lackadaisical loop, as little images seem to replay bit by bit. Why do I feel anxious about these memories? It's as if I'm rationalizing. Have I been crying? I wipe my left cheek, wet from either perspiration or sorrow. I focus back on this room. Where am I? *CLICK*. I'm in an Arth house. Yes. *CLICK*. I live with a host clan in an implanted commune. Yes. Well, I did. Before something . . . something happened on this day that changed all of that. Yes, but what?

Suddenly I hear, "Sonder Light, my child!" Commander? Is that him? Still held in this emotional state, I do not move as he ducks down through the draped curtain in front of what I grasp is a hidden doorway. "I heard the news. Congratulations! I hovered right over and orbited down as quickly as I could. I bring to you a warm Universal Nation acknowledgment for your exponential self-discovered completions! You, my dear, have just set a galactic record for completing four levels almost simultaneously. In completing empathy, creativity, inspiration, and—"

I quickly roll 90 degrees from my back to my side to face him. I know now that they are tears, as my eyes well up again and heat flashes over my whole face. The disparity of our emotions is evident to Commander; he stops himself right there. I haven't a clue what took place this morning, but it must have been big considering Commander was sent here. I haven't seen him in months. Before I can demand answers, I take notice of his apparel. It is unbearably hot, and for some reason, Commander looks to have dressed himself in hopes of experiencing heat exhaustion. The sight of him makes the water in my eyes retract. On this triple-digit day, he wears an official service uniform with matching billed hat. Seeing him I nearly forget my unknown sorrows . . . *nearly.*

I almost ask him to take off his restricting khaki jacket, knowing he must be boiling from the trapped heat generated from his skin suit. Nearly, but not quite. I almost ask him to repeat what four levels I completed in one Arth day, but again, something holds me back. I almost do a lot of things that would remove me from the center of this conversation, but I do not. I am feeling emotionally charged and in need of attention.

Feeling disturbed now that I only hear my thoughts, I roar out telepathically, "*Commander. This is all happening way too fast! This ability to jump back and forth is not easy to keep straight! I know this might not make much sense, but . . . I have no idea where I am in life, why I am so upset, or why you chose to dress like that on a day like this! I'm grateful you're here, but I might not be . . . I might not be here much longer.*"

Laughter causes me to stop whimpering. I wait patiently until Commander is satisfied with his extensive laugh. I don't feel embarrassed or ashamed of my current emotional state in front of Commander. Some might be intimidated by his current status: tall, cut, very stern looking, with the reputation as the most strict faculty member in Spacer University; but I see beyond his Arth skin suit to his squishy Maresan form.

Commander's powerful, but for Ariyan and myself, he is our protective god-guardian first and foremost. He's clan. He served in many battles with Apollo, and was one of the first to start up the Spacers Program with our guardians. I've known Commander this entire lifetime. I always laved his visits between his Zero Zone trips. Often, when we would host gatherings at our home on Mares, or road trips on

Arth, he would join. He relished in reenacting some incredible 'coming of level' tales, which I never heard the ends to before falling asleep. Now more than ever, I could really go for one of the stories, but I don't think that is what I'm going to get.

Commander removes his hat, allowing four beads of sweat to run straight down his face. He takes his right hand to wipe his brow upwards, slicking back his hat hair. He chooses to leave on his jacket as he proceeds, "Sonder, your honesty and innocent demeanor are breath-taking. I do apologize for laughing, but your dramatic words remind me of how emotional young huemans are when present to their own greatness. You are correct; you will not be *here* much longer."

I return my focus to the ceiling fan. Does he know I'm just visiting this memory? What greatness is he talking about? He walks to a desk and chair on the opposing wall from the door. From the corner of my eye, I see him place his hat on the table, pick up the single chair and bring it to my feet.

Commander nonchalantly leans back and begins speaking in an inquisitive tone. "Today, you utilized your aura reader, and that is radiant! Your instincts must have been going wild. To have seen, not only the world, but the connection felt by all the living creatures of this overpopulated planet. This is a rare rite of passage."

FLASH. I appear standing outside, wearing the same clothes. Was this earlier today? I see huge mountains caught in a blazing purple fire. Ariyan seems unsure about his words. His face reads bewildered excitement. I am too choked up and don't speak. My bottom lip quivers and I begin to blubber. I zoom forward to a small squirrel running inside of my head. Something seems off. This squirrel is running in terror. Without saying it, I feel it pleading for help. How can I help? I can't even help myself! Suddenly, the squirrel catches on fire! So does Ariyan! This is a terrible memory to visit. Wretched! Why did this come back to me?

FLASH. My back springs off the floor and I'm greeted by a wide-eyed Commander. He wipes his forehead sweat back into his damp hair and continues, "That rodent was asking the universe for help, and so the universe placed you in its path. What an extraordinary performance you executed. And with your rapid ascensions while training with Ariyan, I am astonished that I didn't see this coming sooner!"

Commander chuckles, "And it's quite common to experience anxiety when accessing the ability to jump back and forth—advanced skills like this are not easy to navigate . . . without proper supervision, you see."

CLICK. Oh, Allah! Commander now knows I'm visiting my past memories. I let him finish, "I'm sure whoever told you about vessel projecting warned you about the intensity you might experience as you activate and navigate within it. Pray tell, who taught you how to engage your aura reader and how to enter that fat rat? Curious, was it Ariyan—did he tell you? Does he often give you direction, or inside pointers?"

I am taken aback by Commander's inquiry. Is that what this ability to jump into memories is called? Vessel projecting? No, I don't think so. Maybe he's not talking about my ability to hop back into these memories. Perhaps he doesn't know that I'm reliving this memory; how would he? Thinking back to my conversation with the pixelated beings, they had mentioned vessel projecting.

CLICK That last memory I had about the squirrel. *CLICK*. Is that the rat Commander is referring to? Oh, no. Does that make me a hypocrite? I hopped into another's body, yet I am so defensive about my own—no, the squirrel asked for help. It gave me permission. Wait, did it? Did I enter its vessel? I try to draw on the incident, but cannot.

I now rest my arms across my knees. I sense this is not to be an ordinary visit by Commander.

Nonetheless, I enjoy his presence. I answer based on what I know. "Oh, Commander. You know me more than most. I assure you, I still have no idea what I'm discovering at this point. Yes, I know of vessel projecting, but to my knowledge, the squirrel came to me . . . I did not seek it out. I only know that the squirrel in my head asked for help—otherwise I wouldn't have been able to do a vessel projection; consent must be given before permitted to enter a vessel. At least that's how I think vessel projection works. Is it?"

Commander seems to be studying my answers. He clears his throat. "Ah, forget I asked. I shall see to it that Ariyan's name is cleared, and that he's rewarded for his assistance in making history. He seemed to have thought that I had taught you about vessel projecting, but clearly you are teaching me something new. Consent might've been overlooked within the curriculum."

I am grateful to have been able to clear Ariyan's name, and desire further clarification, "And what's aura reading? I self-activated a strange glow; Ariyan appeared too scared to explain anything to me."

Commander waves his hand, "Oh, it's nothing for you to concern yourself with at this level." Perhaps he's not, but I am. I just saw my world caught on fire! I lay it out, "With all due respect, I believe I might be a danger to others in my current state of being. I need real help. The kind of help that understands and can control these bizarre abilities; and I need the help now."

Commander flutters his eyelashes, "Are you asking to join Spacer University early?" A bit shocked, I could see how it might seem like that.

I clarify while remaining humble, "Oh, no, Sir! I would cringe if other spacers thought you were favoring me based on biased circumstances. And I am still about seven levels away from the minimum thirty. I know exceptions have been made, but for prana with more merit than I. I just meant—"

My eye contact drifts, but is brought back as Commander's index finger touches my nose. "Sonder, you catapulted up by four levels in one day! It is well-known that you are still at level twenty-seven, still out of range by the old standards, but the modified program now accepts those with promising potential to complete their initial thirty levels prior to reaching Arth's atmosphere. Knowing what you have done in less than an Arth's year here, you show enough potential to be teaching a course by the time we return."

His tone deepens. "And you are quite promising, Sonder. Why, you have already executed aura reading and channeling another's vessel prior to reaching level thirty-one. Frankly, until you . . . well, it was unheard of. Typically, prana do not even become curious about working with other aura levels until mastering a certain level of maturity—roughly around levels thirty-one to thirty-four. You tipped your self-awareness very quickly. In Spacer's training, we introduce this skill prematurely, under the oath that they will not teach or talk about it to anyone who is unaware of the ability, some still cannot activate their readers, and very few can vessel project—you know I don't even know if Ariyan has done one successfully."

Commander leans forward. "Knowing that you are well under level thirty"—he raises his eyebrow— "and if Ariyan really did not leak these secrets"—his face brightens up—"then you are redefining our known universal order." Now I get the weight of this situation, but I am confused about this oath of secrecy.

Raising my eyebrow, I ask, "Commander, isn't it hypocritical for the Universal Nation to make a rule that only the UN faculty are allowed to break?"

Commander becomes befuddled as I continue, "I mean, why would the program make a rule that spacers cannot teach prana beings this developmental skill, knowing that the faculty break their oath once the new spacers promise not to do what the UN goes ahead and does? Sounds like an educational perversion in hopes of holding power."

Commander looks a bit uneasy, before asking a counter-question. He gestures his hands toward me, "You might ask yourself the same thing about yourself someday, if you become a master at Spacer University. It's easy to have all the questions but not as such to be asked for all the answers. I mean," he looks at me with discernment, "your morality only allows you to see one way, because it's fixed in a linear order of correctness."

Commander closes his eyes and opens them with great pride, "If your biggest challenge is that you have only been seeing life one way, consider your life easy! Your lessons are not as hard as most. On top of that, you have always been advanced. Your ability to detect fallacies is powerful, and your morality finds hypocrisy effortlessly. Soon, you will surpass most of your superiors . . . even Ariyan. You do it genuinely, while exuding endless amounts of curiosity, love, and connection unknowingly. How is it that you completely ignore this?"

There's no denying it, I never thought about my capability to surpass prana beings that were born before me . . . at least not those closest to me.

Commander then asks a question I never thought about: "Tell me, do you think yourself capable of surpassing Ariyan on levels, or will you always see him more advanced?"

Smoothing down his shirt, as if he didn't ask that last question, he continues. "You bring up a solid point. Our practices could be seen as hypocritical in that we only provide knowledge to those who promise to be responsible with the education we give them in a safe environment. We know that most that have activated their aura readers or vessel project outside of the university have experienced states of hysteria. We don't want to risk it happening anymore, so we allocate control settings and implement restraints. But what about your restraints? Similar to Cassiopeia, you talk up and help out all those around you, but do not pay this same respect to yourself."

Commander looks down for a moment, then back at me, "You wholeheartedly give unto others, but to give to yourself seems like a challenge. Spacer University will facilitate your allevelation with sages and masters to help hone in your craft. I recognize that your connection to the rodent must've been a call for help—from you. In our program, you will get that help." He rests his chin on the palm of his right hand that is supported by his knee, then hunches toward me, "Perhaps that is why I am really here. Not as a recruiter, but as a connector. A connector between you and your higher self." I nod as he continues, "Spacer University creates communities, where spacers work among huemans on Arth. All present are willing to function as contributions during the gatherings. It is a space with no competition, just collaboration. We are all in service to the flowing universe, whether we oppose or approve."

In that moment, I *FLASH* to a memory where Cassiopeia is cupping my face in her hands and recites: "Prana in service are best at serving when they do not feel like servants." The memory dissipates.

I return focus to Commander, who divulges, "These events take place in different climatic regions and different durations throughout Arth's calendar. The newest site: Zero Zone. It occurs in a location that very closely resembles Mares' climate and atmosphere. Yes, these events will have you truly experience what it's like to help others let go of what is holding them back, and in return for your services, you'll gain the wisdom most will never know. You'll learn how to guide others through transcendence. So many of these Arthlings come to Zero Zone wanting to transcend—they might even beg, like your fat little squirrel; but it's not enough to want it . . . they need to need it. That's where we come in."

I'm not quite following. "You come in for what? What are spacers expected to do at Zero Zone that has sleepers want to need something?"

Commander seems to recite, "That will be answered in training . . . but in short, we prepare you to be in the left space with the left mind to best serve those in the right place at the right time."
This sounds like a riddle. I blurt out, "But how will I know when that is? And what if I'm not in the right mind?"

A bit cheekily, Commander says, "I said your left mind, not the right. And with that attitude, I don't know if you'll ever get there." Retracting his tone, he encourages, "Even if that's the case, no worries. That will be answered in training . . ."

Commander knows I'm skeptical; he adds, "Look, the truth is that the current state of Arth is stagnant; too many Arthlings are questioning if they are going to make the right move, and these stoppages are building up. The prana on Arth wants to be released, but it doesn't know how to get relief. I get what you are concerned about—I've felt it more times than I'd like to admit . . . This mission is daunting, because you have to trust that by becoming a spacer it will make a difference before you can know anything. You have to believe that when the time comes for action, you will have the necessary mindset to lead others. Trust me, I get it. As the Recruitment Chair, it pains me the most when advanced young Regins like yourself used to ask for help in wanting access to this training, I'd have to turn them away . . . until now."

Commander claps his hands together. "Recently, I submitted an appeal to our program and got approved to expand the program's acceptance for spacers in the upcoming Zero Zone 2045 A.D. We will match the numbers deployed in Africa; three hundred spacers will board. This doubles my recruitment numbers! And all are necessary for waking this region of Arthlings. If we make contact with sleepers outside of these implanted communes, in order to make an impact, it has to be at Zero Zone. Just knowing there is a higher level of being doesn't benefit you if you cannot bring yourself to a higher level of thinking. I fear us integrating these communes has hindered their lives. By not deriving their own applications, they only copy, never create. Arthlings easily adapt to technical advances, but grow hostile with thoughts of unknown enhancements . . ."

Not certain, I feel Commander has an ulterior motive. Why is he bringing this up? He looks around the room, "I thought I was doing my duty as a god-guardian to give you a stable environment while Spacer University was in session, but I fear that once the new program begins, and Ariyan comes back with me, I would be neglecting you by having you remain within the communes. True, I think you will like the next one picked out for you, but I really want the best for you."

I look around the room and I'm curious why he uses the word neglect. A fuzzy image of what looks like a dinner table.

FLASH. I see bowls and cups are placed for a clan of four. I see Ariyan, but jerk my attention toward another fuzzy body that seems to be pointing at me in an accusing manner. What did I do? Why do I feel like I did something that was upsetting? I panic and look back toward Ariyan, who also shows disdain toward me. I want to escape this wretched memory as well. I shake my head.

FLASH. Looking at the door that Commander came through, I'm convinced that the wretched memory took place recently. Right outside that draped doorway. Suddenly, without remembering what took place, I no longer wish to stay here.

Commander explains, "These implanted communes we helped build have become more toxic than the planted communes that spore out of nowhere. These communes have become

107

nightmares that the inhabitants refuse to wake from. These metal walls boarding their homes, hotels, and hospitals have become hospice cocoons giving no motivation to break out—more inhuemane than the savages living outside these silo walls; out in the planted communes. I know your host family means well, but they fear rejection and cling to praise, like pets in a cage trying to please their master in hopes of escaping this reality. A reality beyond their cage . . . but I fear by choosing a life inside this cage, their minds will now cease to fly once freed from their skin cells." He sighs once more. I feel his sympathy. Clearing his throat, and turning up his authoritative tone, "What I am proposing is for you to join the Spacer University Training Program for the Zero Zone mission."

"Oh my Allah . . . is this happening to me? Wait, you already knew you go to Zero Zone 2045. You're reliving a memory. Just focus."

He proceeds with unwavering intention. "As a Spacer, you will represent the Mares community. There are many representatives you will encounter— other extraterrestrials from different planets, light liaisons from moons—and you will be trained and educated by our experienced sages and masters. You will be groomed to be able to engage with any derivative of hueman being encountered while on Arth."

I lean back to readjust as Commander holds up two fingers. "There are two types of hueman beings you will run into out here: hueman beings like your host clan that have tapped into the mass consciousness; and those who have not. Those who have not outnumber those who have. Those who have not tapped in avoid responsibility and depend on society, simply by overindulging and finding blame in others."

I think back on this host clan that he claims to being tapped in who were yelling at me. How can that be? Did my memory deceive me? Is it possible to be tapped in, and still blame others?

I hold on to this thought, as Commander lays out the rest of it, "Prana who blame others often seem to see Zero Zone as a ticket to get away from something; they seek to escape. They want to run to a place where they believe others are supposed to take care of them, but that is not Zero Zone's intention. It can seem like that, but it is much more for those who see the opportunity to grow and help others. Not everyone is ready, which is fine; we only help prana beings that are willing to move on. Our mission is to connect with those who desire to be free."

Still skeptical, I ask, "How do you know they want to be freed?"

Commander seems to humor me as he responds, "I said desire, not want. You can never help someone who wants something. Wants are quickly replaced with more wants; leaving prana beings exactly where they were. It has to be something that they desire, or know they need; there lies the hidden momentum that propels life forward. It's easy to spot with a bit of practice. And that will be answered in training . . . Honestly, I have full faith that anyone who completes the Spacer Program will be prepared for any and all sleepers."

Commander stares at me, and only continues once he is sure I understand what he said, "Yes, it has been known that the emotional hueman being is the most powerful being when aligned with their own divinity. Arthlings are easily derailed because of this same emotional power. It has been said that they may redefine what it means to be connected with the universe, but only after being guided by spacers. And you too will be ready to have these types of impactful conversations . . . if you join us, instead of creating upset as you did out there." He motions toward the draped curtain with a disappointed look.

I feel ashamed. Wishing to be impactful, I inquire, "How do I join you?"

Without skipping a beat, Commander informs me, "By coming with me. I already completed your board acceptance hearing this morning for this upcoming spacer training program. I approved of you. I am confident in your ability to complete beyond the thirty required levels before returning to Arth."

Hearing this causes me to initiate unwavering excitement. I squeak out, "Are you saying I should—I mean, I'm already permitted to join? This is what I've always wanted!" I have an overwhelming amount of gratitude toward this program even though I know this is just a memory.

Commander chuckles at my reaction, "Now Sonder, this is a huge responsibility to be called upon to serve before a certain level of experience has been mastered. Usually, spacers joining us have one or two levels to master; if you have not reached level thirty before dawn on the last training day, I will order you to stay on the ship—affirmative?"

Without hesitation, I continuously nod; this is what I wanted. Commander repeats, "Affirmative?"

I cue in, "Affirmative, Sir." I stop the moment I feel doubt. It must have been painted on my face.

Like always, Commander sets my worries to ease, "Ahhh . . . to be given freedom to do what you desire, only to realize you do not know what to do with this freedom. Well, that is the beauty of our work. Spacer University allows you to discover not only what you want, but actually what you need—through the listening of others. This mission will speak to you, as it speaks to all, if you listen. In my completion, I discovered a great peace internally after my first mission, but only through my service as a spacer. By Allah, it transformed my entire existence. That is what I want for you."

Why did he say want? I ask skeptically, "What if I do not discover what I actually need by the time I am to depart and begin my mission?"

Commander raises his eyebrow. "Sonder, my dear, everything is in divine order. In the words of Cassiopeia: 'Everything's done with absolute divinity; If it doesn't happen, it wasn't meant to be.'" He winks, "You will be ready for your mission when your time comes." He smiles and slaps his knee. "Who knows—you might stay on the ship, and your time might not come until the next Zero Zone!" We both laugh.

111

Commander wipes his brow's sweat and licks his dry lips before concluding, "You will have to become a little more mentally tough, Sonder, my dear. Huemans reflect some nasty things. Their self-worth can be pretty low sometimes. You cannot take it personally, when their conviction of you being less than them shows; racism is real to them." I remember when Ariyan marked the hueman race with doom and damnation. Was it because they disturbed his secure grounding? If only he were to practice sympathy like Commander in his observations, instead of letting it fester his foundation.

Commander stands, revealing that sweat has now seeped through his shirt and onto his outer jacket, "Just keep in mind, you are being recruited to help these primitive beings, who are sensitive about their desensitized lifestyles. They can become very defensive when questioned."

Pointing to his mouth, he says, "That's why we listen to their words." Now pointing to his heart, he adds, "But we reflect from their worlds. When you are supporting someone who is on the edge of altering their mindset, the magic comes from observing and acknowledging that prana's point of view without degrading or lessening the importance they mark it with." He takes the chair back to its original location and retrieves his hat.

Commander walks back over to my feet, and then places his hat on his head. "There is nothing you can teach. You can only echo what you hear, because they will only hear their own self-reflection.

Just act as the mirror they are seeking; that is all. It will take some practice; I know you will practice."

Commander now straightens up at attention. I snap up with my hands to my sides as he concludes, "By choosing to participate in this program, do you declare yourself as someone who will follow through with the mission, reliably listen, and always return the communication without persuasion, manipulation, or alteration?"

I nod and declare, "I am of service."

Commander smirks, "Excellent. Congratulations on your acceptance. Pack your things; we're off to Spacer University."

6 RADIANT QUESTIONS

Flash—Huzzah!

I vividly remember the entirety of that last conversation with Commander, but what's left to be uncovered leading up to that conversation? Something earlier that day; Commander said something about a rodent. Did it all have to do with that squirrel I visualized running to me for help? What was an aura reader? He didn't really explain that . . . Is that how I see those glowing orbs?

Let's see. I try activating this aura reader; nothing. I look at my pixelated appendage, focus, and . . . nothing. I throw my appendages down in frustration. Maybe I'm not mature enough . . . now.

This is too slow of a process. I sit up and look around the dormitory, hoping to spark a memory of some sort. Nothing seems to leap out. I sink a bit into the bed.

I think back on my last two flashbacks, in hopes of figuring out why those memories came back to me. Let's see—Ariyan was teaching me the ropes, as he often did, but who told him he shouldn't have teled me on the day of my birth, and was it that guilt alone that had him take on training me? He seems to take the blame a lot. Even Commander seemed to accuse Ariyan of showing me that aura reading thing. Was I the reason Ariyan was always being made to feel wrong?

"Radiant questions," Contralto adds.

I look around the room and inter-com, *"Are you ever going to answer any of my questions?"* No response. I take that as a no. I continue to ask questions without expecting answers.

What else stood out? I tele to the unseen pixelated beings, *"Oh! Ariyan's self-worth! He constantly doubted himself in comparison to our guardians. I speculate that his feelings about his teachings reflect his emotional Arthling Self. Commander said Arthlings are the most powerful emotional beings, and so it would make me assume that anytime an Arthling feels powerless in practice, it could be an early sign they're just derailed. Do you agree?"*

"Enlightening and insightful questions," Bass assures.

I'd much rather have a response of yes or no, but I take Bass's response as assurance I am on the left track. *CLICK*. Now, back to Commander. What was incomplete about our conversations? It seemed straightforward; except the hypocrisy. It almost seemed like he was avoiding my questions with many tangents. Why though? He always answered my questions. What questions didn't Commander answer? I take a deep breath.

CLICK. Why did they alter the acceptance for the program? And why was there a hearing for my acceptance in the program, before even discussing it with me?

Affirmations from Baritone, "_Ah! Such profound questions._"

"No help from you!" I squawk out.

SNAP. I really love that they just listen to all of my questions. It feels as though they are intruding on my mind. I begin to tele, _"What did Commander know about my allevelation that he was not telling me? And why does the Universal Nation make spacers take that stupid oath of secrecy?"_

Bass teles, _"That part of history might not be important. What is important is to resolve the questions that you can complete for your Self. Be mindful of the emotion that your questions are rooted in."_ Sounds accurate.

CLICK. I cannot begrudge someone without understanding what direction their intention is in. Commander has always wanted the best for me, and whether or not there is more to the story, he is not here to entertain my wild after-thought questions. My desire was to join Spacer University; fortunately for me, Commander had expanded and expedited the acceptance process, and believed that I was not helped in reading auras—even though it seemed far-fetched from universal truth. He took a risk on me, with telling the truth and meeting the requirements in time. If anything, I should have thanked—oh, no! Did I ever thank Commander for what he did for me?

CLICK!

"_Radiant question!_" Soprano exclaims. How could I have been so selfish? *SNAP*. Wait, I still have time. I always have time!

CLICK. They might be memories, but I can still complete incomplete conversations within them. I'll look for a later conversation, and pick up back up with Commander. I pick up MIT, and flip open to the back of the book. It is blank—the whole latter half is not used. Drats.

I look through the book in reverse order until I find the last page that has an entry. Three very short paragraphs were written September 23, 2045. Before reading the last entry, I pinch all the used pages with my pixelated appendage. I look at the amount of pages, and realize that this is my only hope of revealing everything about Sonder. The entirety of my past takes place in such a small amount of space. I let the moment pass and return to the last entry:

Salutations MIT -

What a whirlwind of events. It all seems like a blur, until Ethan took off during the "Time Keeper" bonfire—such a lovely experience of free-flowing prana beings. It didn't mean anything that he left me like that. I'm grateful that it happened . . . Sincerely, I mean, not in the exact moment, but once Ethan took off, I felt free . . . and in that freedom, I found myself enlivened with Eve, Thoth, and Gabriel. Such magic happened yesterday afternoon, after my conversation with Ariyan, our epic kar-ma-

wash, and meeting Gabriel. What looked like another solo watchtower evening turned into one of my favorite sonder sighting dates!

Today seems a bit cloudy, but I know that it will most likely burn off for another extraordinary bonfire tonight! I wonder if Gabriel will still want to sit with me. Regardless, I will be thinking about all the ways we connected, and the feeling of falling asleep next to him. We just had such great conversations of affinity!

I just noticed Commander sitting in our camp watchtower ever so peacefully. I am so grateful for everything that he has done for me. I am going to go join him—today is the best day I have ever experienced; and it is, because I said so!

Eve! *CLICK*. My roomie! I turn to look at the resting unit next to me with every blanket folded perfectly. She was the youngest spacer in universal history to join the program. Eve—oh, my Eve! Also known as Every. She was my best friend. And Thoth, who grew very sweet on Eve—I remember them!

Who are Ethan and Gabriel though? And what is sonder sighting about? I close MIT, and my mind begins to wander a bit. I will discover who I am. I close out the awareness to the light in the room and retreat into a state as if I am going to sleep. I feel it, almost like I can drift off; I'm right on the edge . . . and nothing. I begin to allow the light of the room to filter back into my awareness.

As I do, the high-frequency voice echoes the phrase, **_"Try as you might, you cannot wake those who are pretending to sleep."_** I sit up and look around the room, pondering if I am being criticized for my attempt to jump ahead in my self-discover-me journey. Wait . . . Who am I being judged or mocked by? This is my inner intelligence talking. And I'm just attempting to *try* different methods of returning to memories. Even if it only produces a failure. Perhaps I am not to force things, but there is no shame in me attempting new things.

CLICK. I cross it off as an ineffective way of recalling memories. There is no forcing them to come. There, no failure—truly a success in rediscovering myself. Self-discovery is a journey not to be forced; it should be enjoyed, as it comes to me. *CLICK*. This journey is a game! And I am rediscovering the enjoyment that occurs when one waits for life to happen through the ebbing-and-flowing cycle. I lie back once more with this reclaimed peace of mind.

As for the other two—Ethan and Gabriel—I am sure they will come back to me. Yes, when I am ready to discover them again. **More confident in my current state**, I return to MIT. I skim toward the middle of my journal entries. I stop on August 1, 2034:

Salutations MIT -

I just completed my first projection into a sleeper, down here in Zion! Oh what a joy!

Ariyan and I are heading back in the hover vehicle now to go see our host family. Oh, lucky me! He said that this might be big enough news that Apollo and Cassiopeia might come back from their MAD mission, so we can celebrate! Ariyan is informing everyone he can think of on our way back to the Bivit's home, and all I'm doing is writing in you! You should feel pretty special, MIT. Just kidding!

It felt a bit like a dream. Ariyan and I were walking through the shrubs by the base of Angel's Landing, and all of a sudden I looked at Ariyan, who began to get a—

The memory starts rushing back to me. I quickly lie MIT down on my chest as the memory returns to me. This is what I have been waiting for! The memory that is going to bring it all back to me. Slowly, the room begins to fade out—here it comes.

MIT — THE ROCK SQUIRREL

FLASH. I'm surrounded by bleak darkness. Slowly, light begins filtering in. I can see Ariyan's head bobbing up and down. Then the rest of his body becomes present, and then—oh, my!

I was not ready for all of this. How could I have forgotten this? The vivid memory was not done justice by the few jots of words I formulated into MIT. I hadn't even mentioned anything of this visual masterpiece. It's unreal.

It was as if a professional team came in and decorated the entire scene by hand to give the illusion that something naturally could form so effortlessly, and be left with such a modest term simply called, "the outdoors"!

A vastly rich array of lush spruces of green can be seen throughout the entire canvas of giant rock formations surrounding us. I have to catch my breath at first glance, still off-guard. What a magnificent sight to become present in! I should listen to my own advice more often: this journey doesn't need to be forced, simply enjoyed as it comes. Mountains fold in and out of one another with rich warm tones of marbled colors that remind me of Mares.

Mares. I forgot what it looks like. I forgot that the greatest treasure of any planet is in exploring and experiencing its unexplainable beauty. I remember now. My childish smile begins on my face, and it radiates throughout my body—so this is what it feels like when starlight glisters from within. I look up, and let go of figuring out my past— while being completely in this moment, I become light, and so does everything around me. *CLICK*. Huzzah! I activate the aura reader!

The rocks, clouds, and surrounding greenery all flicker and dance in vibrant hues of violet and lavender! It's activated by being light seeking light!

CLICK. How fascinating. I easily spot prana beings making their way up the mountain and ones standing around—even through bushes. All the Arthlings are different beams of sky blue, lime green, and seldom canary yellow light. I yelp, which turns into a wail once I see this has happened to Ariyan as well. He is covered in a teal blue sheen! Ariyan jerks back to me, very guarded, "What? What's happening, Sonder? Errr—uh, Susun."

He regains his composure. "Are you okay? Not feeling up for the hike today?"

I shake my head. Almost begging, "Then, what is it, Sonder?" I hold out my right index finger directly at him, then jump back when I discover that I too am covered in color—a magnificent shade of cerulean blue which excites me as much as it frightens me. I frantically try wiping off the sheen from my right hand; it doesn't budge.

Ariyan grabs for my right hand, blocking my left hand from rubbing, causing all beams of light to shut off. I look at the surrounding travelers, now staring at me in wonder. They carry no judgement as they continue on their hike. I look back at Ariyan, who sounds concerned, "Get a hold of yourself. Now, what—"

I spew out words, "LIGHTS! Eve'ywhere! On you, and 'dem, and the moundens, and me! I—" I pull my right hand back into a ball safe inside my left. I compose myself and articulate clearly, "I was just surprised. That's all. I thought it was going to be harder to read auras. Commander made it seem impossible on my level. I was caught off guard. That's all."

Ariyan looks mesmerized, "No way! You can read aura!? How did you . . . When did Commander even talk to you about this?" He begins wildly questioning me, with great glee. I do not hear most of his questions, as I start to question my own sequence of events. I only knew of aura reading after talking with Commander. But this moment must have happened before then; otherwise, that conversation would have never taken place.

Suddenly, Cassiopeia's jingle rings clear: Everything's done with absolute divinity; If it doesn't happen, it wasn't meant to be.

I refocus on this present and catch the end of what Ariyan is saying, "Susun, how are you such a winner at the game of life?" He starts laughing again. "Well, I'm not supposed to speak about levels I'm mastering outside of university, but as a responsible peer, I cannot just withhold information when it could help you! You are clearly ready for it, and without proper spacer program guidance, you could slip into hysteria!" He winks at me, which returns me to a calmer state.

"Okay, let's take a seat," Ariyan instructs and I follow his lead. We take a few steps off the path, cross our legs, and face each other. Ariyan goes right to it, "Everywhere in the galaxy contains prana. All forms of prana in life radiate a certain frequency based on its level of openness; that's what you just saw.

Depending on the level of openness, it appears to illuminate different auras. Plants and rocks will always radiate the highest violet aura, because it's rarely affected by anything emotionally and it is almost always open to flow at any time. They are pretty constant, so for now, you can ignore them." He pauses, "Sentient objects are a bit tricky, because potential openness alters based on their current states of connection, and comfort with their surroundings."

I look around at the violets and lavenders, then at the sky blues, lime greens, and so on. I lift up my right hand, still teal, and ask, "Is blue gewd?"

Ariyan playfully slaps my hand down, "Did I say GOOD or bad?" My right hand is now green. I shake my head, feeling embarrassed. Ariyan, sounding

124

exhausted, continues, "I'm teasing you, kid. I apologize for the way it came across to you."

I shake it off, and keep learning unapologetically. "Blue indicates a prana's willingness to connect is at a high potential. Not as high as purple, but higher than, let's say, a prana in a state of kelly green—and much higher than rosy-red."

He looks me up and down. "You're an emotional roller coaster! One moment, you're blue, then green. A moment ago you were teal; now you've returned to a vocal blue. Again, we fluctuate. Some more than others. The way I interact is always on my toes. I try not to disconnect. Now that you know, I will never leave you too long before finding a way to reconnect." Ariyan holds his left hand with the palm facing me and continues, "I promise." I hold up my right hand to his. I nod, knowing he never makes promises; this feels nice.

Ariyan laces his left hand's fingers between mine, pushes himself up with his right hand, and then pulls me up. He takes a deep breath, and teles, *"Close your eyes and focus on your heartbeat. Feel the warmth in the palm of my hand. Now, feel the coolness of my fingertips on the back of your hand."* I close my eyes, but don't want to see all the lights again—no more melted kaleidoscope, please. He walks me through it. *"Focus on the warmth, so when you open your eyes, the warmth will be focused on you. Find all the warmth that surrounds you; connect your warmth as one."* He squeezes my hand, and I can feel his warmth; I feel the coolness of his fingertips. I am still hesitant to open my eyes, but at this moment, I do not need to.

With my eyes closed, I start feeling the warmth of all the surroundings! My warmth yearns to be close to all of the prana around me. Even though I do not see their auras, I definitely feel them; they are very welcoming. I finally open my eyes and gain connection to all of the spruces, the shrubs and small trees, the rocks and clouds. All are flickering and dancing in their brilliant hues of violet and lavender.

Birds flying above and clusters of prana making their way up the path beam with sky blues, lime greens, and a few canary yellows. It's like watching a beautiful painting in motion. Saturated color schemes appear in obscure locations. Wait; is it obscure to see purple clouds, or blue hueman beings? Also, is it weird that most of the hueman beings around here seem much happier than the ones claiming to be normal while cooping themselves up in our neighborhood, and never leave their silo? In fact, what is normal? I let out a blissful sigh and look back at Ariyan, still holding my hand. We are both violet.

Ariyan squeezes my hand. "How do you feel now, Susun? You want to continue forward on our hike?" With great joy I respond, "Affirmative!"

We return to the path and approach the trailhead marker. I continue to watch the auras, and play around with filtering certain auras in and out. As we walk toward the restrooms, I remove the awareness of the rocks and plants; I return the visible restroom to its painted state. I can still see the radiated auras of all the people and animals.

126

I make a playful observation, "Hey, Adrian. Don't you think it's funny that the prana going into the restroom are in close ranges of oranges, but as they come out, they are within the green or more opened ranges?"

He puts his arm around me, and begins to give me a noogie, "Well, missy. Looks like someone is very observant."

I escape his grasp and almost fling myself into the trash container placed right outside the trailhead. As I dodge the canister, I can hear rattling from inside of it. I get a bit closer, and see a bushy, amber-colored tail swishing the surrounding wrappers and plastic bottles; it's a very round squirrel. It stops rummaging, looks at me, and without a moment's notice, starts pulling itself out of the can. This squirrel acquired the longing for hueman food, like most creatures near the park. I knew it craved the edibles of the highest temptation: chips. I pick up on its frustrations and confusion about its current habitual loop that has left it in a poor physical state, slumped over and waddling. It lacks any motivation to forage for food, knowing any and all nearby metal canisters have bounties of food readily available and already collected for its convenience. With rational thinking like that, why wouldn't it always go for the supplied sustenance? It's common sense in modern society's thinking to stay; but I feel it reaching out to me.

CLICK. This is the squirrel that was in my head. It's scrambling to become free of the canister. Without diving into the complexity of a ground squirrel's morality, I know its desire to be set free from

127

its dependency loop. It knows its dependency on the metal container has stopped it from going forth in its game of life. Commander was right; it did find me.

CLICK. I look back at Ariyan with arms crossed and chin raised. I return back to the squirrel, who has pulled itself out of the trash and cautiously approached me.

With no further thought of the matter, I begin to empathize with this native creature, first wishing for it to grant me consent to help it. How do I know if it'll give me permission? I don't speak squirrel. *CLICK*. Arth's universal body language! I crouch down to its level, and before I know it, I'm literally projected into a life of a stealthy and agile squirrel. It's as if I have spent my whole life scurrying through the rocks and shrubbery, gathering delicious white pine seeds from the desert ground. I want to connect with other squirrels now. I get to explore this rocky terrain from the viewpoint of a squirrel. It feels great. After scurrying through the woods, I find myself heading back to a canister. I now face a dilemma.

There is a want to return to the easy circle tower that provides me with cheap snacks and scraps, but I would rather have my trees and friends. Thinking about returning to the highest branches of the trees, I'm left with no desire to climb back to the trash collector. I had my fill of seeds, and was fully satisfied. I can feel the longing for chips dissipate as I begin thinking more and more about the pine seeds and a sense of reclaiming my old . . . sunbathing rock.

Suddenly, a slab of granite pops into my head. Strange—what sunbathing rock? The more I think about it, the more I can't believe I forgot about the almighty rock. This rock that must have been gifted to me by Allah himself! I shall return right away! I turn away from the canister, and become startled to now be looking up at myself—the me, that is Susun.

Susun is down on all fours. A few people walk by, and do nothing besides snicker. This vessel-projecting experience is a bit intense. I am not just any squirrel; I entered memories and became *this* squirrel.

Looking past my body, I see Ariyan just staring at me—the me that is Susun. He looks a bit concerned, which I do not like. I try to ease his mind by saying, *"Yan, I am alright. I just need to go find my rock, and—"*

Now he is looking at me—the me that is the squirrel. His eyes go wild. He calls out, "Susun?"

How has this . . .? Am I dreaming? I look back at myself as Susun, and then look back at Ariyan. He stares at me intently. **_"Am I going to be stuck in this squirrel's body?"_**

CLICK. I then chirp and snap back as Susun, shockingly—I now stare dead ahead into the right eye of the squirrel, who's still located in front of me, supported on its hind legs. I begin to stand up, as the squirrel slowly descends down on all fours. I instantly get chills at the sound of Ariyan's applause, causing my head to whip over my shoulder. The warmth I feel from his happiness toward me radiates from his laving smile.

I return my attention to the chubby little turquoise beaming rock squirrel, who has its taste for life back. My newest friend gifts me a grateful bowing motion, before aborting its dependency on the metal canister to scamper off toward the rocks once more. This, for me, is the greatest feeling I've experienced in all twenty-three levels . . . or am I twenty-seven now?

Ariyan embraces me with love and admiration for my accomplishment. He continues on about it during our hike up and back down. He shares with me tips and tricks he learned from Oknotok, which is a course in the spacer program. I blow him away, already figuring out how to abate non-sentient auras.

After our hike, we hop in the hovercraft, and Ariyan sends communication to Apollo and Cassiopeia—no answer. Ariyan pats my hand to assure me he'll try again later. He activates the hovercraft and heads homeward. I feel disappointed that they didn't answer. I know Ariyan feels the same way. We both still have hope. I should be used to their silence after eight months. Wow . . . it's been eight months already. Where has the time gone?

Looking into the distance, I wonder now how far away that sunbathing rock is from here. Maybe that squirrel has offspring to return to . . . I wonder if its offspring were waiting for their guardian's long-last return. Maybe that's why the squirrel found me; to give me hope as I still wait for my guardian's return. Please let that squirrel make it back safely to its sunbathing rock. Please; please, Allah.

MIT — PERPETUAL CATCH 22

I seem to have dozed off. Feeling groggy, I look out the hovercraft's window and see we are nearing two giant trash canisters—err, I mean silos.

This thought is too funny to keep to myself, "Hey, Ariyan. Do you think it's a coincidence that the silos look like giant trash containers?"

Ariyan glances at me sideways "Hey, sleepy head. Sounds like you're still synced with that squirrel's mindset . . . but you're not too far off. Sadly, they do serve the same purpose." I look behind me, hoping to get my bearings. We're halfway back home. These first two communes begin the endless string of metal cans from here on out. Turning forward, I notice two faint tire marks, taking off in a direction heading to the mountains. I never noticed them before.

I point at them, "Do you see those tire marks, Adrian?"

Ariyan looks around. "No. What tire marks?"

I abruptly stop the conversation as we approach the first rows of trees; or should I say dense green wall. I desperately scan the horizon, mountains, and the small uneven wild bushes. Once we hit the road's tree line, my life will be forced back into uniformity until Ariyan returns on his next holiday from Zero Zone. While our guardians are on their MAD mission, I have been assigned by the Universal Nation to remain undercover in a suburban silo lifestyle on Arth. I remind myself it's temporary—and I'm only alone for the months that Ariyan reports for his spacer training.

I hold my breath, as we plunge into the governmental property line. Both sides of the road are lined with thick pinyon pines. I wonder who chose these trees out of the dozens of choices. No sunlight passes through, and they're too tall to see any sign of nature on either side of the road.

We finally hover past the first two mirrored implanted communes, after the rows upon rows of densely grown pinyons, there's a break in the line; only in front of the metal canisters. The only part that is visible on the silo is the opened section for the driveway. Right after the driveway, the densely packed tree line continues. From driveway to driveway—approximately a two-mile stretch between each canister on each side. I shut my eyes to fight the suffocating feeling. Ariyan brings me back sarcastically, "I love what they've done with the trees since I left—on your side of the road, at least. The personality of each tree is unique." I snicker a bit, before I settle into an unspoken sadness. Just like these communes, each tree looks no different than the one before or after it.

I remember when I used to get excited for the long drives. There used to be variety, and we never took the highway—always the backroads. As we near the next set of communes, I grow tiresome thinking of the Arthlings who live inside these walls. I say without thinking, "Cookie cutter, bland as butter." Ariyan seems surprised by my tone, "Yeah . . . I remember what excitement it used to bring you to marvel at all the different skin suits. You remember when there used to be lots of red and black haired Arthlings? You didn't believe me back then; but I showed you."

Now Ariyan adopts a solemn tone, "Nowadays, I guess I would've called myself a liar. Hey, on today's hike, I actually saw skin suits that were your shade—and two huemans with black hair! Allah, they must be hiding." I try not to be sad, knowing that Ariyan is trying to cheer me up. He knows I still struggle emotionally with physically standing out.

It seems like most huemans we see all look like him. Light complexion, straight blonde hair with blue eyes. Unlike Ariyan, who tries to overlook my appearances, these communers let me know I don't belong in their silo. We pass by miles of these densely packed trees and half-a-dozen silo communes, all identical to the one our host family was assigned to.

Ariyan breaks the silence with more conversation, "What do you think is really going on beyond those fortresses of forest walls? Seems like someone went through an awful lot of effort to make it appear like nothing happens between the closed communes."

I squint, trying to look through the branches and trunks. "I never thought about it. I was thinking back on our clan's cross-country road trips, and don't remember these silos or uniformed trees."

Ariyan touches his nose, "That's 'cuz these weren't here. Not even on our last road trip with Cassiopeia and Apollo. They only popped up after they were assigned to this MAD mission. This is why I'm curious what's going on out there. You said you saw a path?" I nod my head. Ariyan speculates, "I wonder where most of those hikers came from today on the trail."

Now I perk up a bit. "Yeah! Did you see how they had dirty shoes and messy hair?"

Ariyan grants me a side smile, "You best believe, little sister. I laved the way they were dressed, and the aura readings I picked up didn't match most of the prana beings in our posh neighborhood. I wonder if those outdoorsy prana came from the outcasted communes that our host clan warned us about. If so, what would you say to exploring a bit more next time? Maybe trying to follow those tire tracks you saw, aye?"

This upcoming adventure thrills me, "Mission accepted!"

Staring forward, Ariyan produces a cheesy grin, "Maybe these outcasts aren't the ones to be feared."

I replay these lasting words, and become really curious why these silos look so fortified. What do they think the outsiders will do? The silos on my side of the road have aluminum walls, while the ones on Ariyan's side have titanium. Like enforced colosseums, they were designed to withstand a break in . . . from a tank. Based on my observations of those living in these implanted communes, they still act as if tanks exist; their mindsets are trembling inside of their mental bunkers. I don't think most of them have ever stepped outside of the silo they were born in. The main road allows for all silos to connect and visit one another, but with each one being identical, there is no need. They never venture outside.

As we pull into our gated driveway to our host family's aluminum silo commune, I feel the judgment seep in all around me. Once I am surrounded by disapproving eyes, I instantly question what I did wrong. "Why do they look at me with disgust? Do they know I'm an alien?"

Ariyan scoffs, "As if these morons could focus on anything beyond the dirt on our vehicle. Good thing. They are so distracted by the dust." He hits a switch, "I hadn't turned on the wheel simulation. We could have three heads, but they're conditioned to get distracted by disgust of organic filth. They've got an incredible cranium processor, but they've dumbed down any anomalies outside of their uniform silos. Don't take it personally that they disdain everything that happens outside of these walls; like living life. I don't know how you've managed it down here for so long." The answer is simple—I have no choice. Sometimes I wish I looked like Ariyan. Maybe then life would be more bearable.

Their menacing eyes don't seem to bother Ariyan, but I cannot stand it. I turn to MIT as Ariyan begins another cheery monologue of what it was like to watch me in action. I am surprised when I have already written this entry. 2034 is the Arth year, yet the next Zero Zone isn't until 2045. I must be missing something. "Hey, Adrian . . . When do you take off for Spacer University?"

He thinks about it as he pulls out of the commercial segment of the commune and begins looping through the residences. "I think tomorrow, or the day after that. Why?"

I knew that. "Yeah, but when do you come back?"

He shakes his head. "It hasn't been assigned a date yet. It's an annual event . . . but they are expanding—I'm guessing 2035." That's what I was thinking. Why did Commander say 2045 A.D.?

Ariyan resumes his monologues as we putter through the commune's spaghetti-like design. Whipping through the street, he sends another communication to Apollo and Cassiopeia. No answer. We reach our house and both silently agree to sit in the hovership a bit longer. Staring blankly into the living room quarters, I can see the Bivits—an interesting pair. Braxton and Amelia always wanted offspring, but couldn't decide if it was better to have a child born with Scorpio rising, or Libra rising. Not able to make up their minds, they still tend an empty nest; hence why they have an extra room. I am thankful that they are more open-minded than most, but for how long?

The United Nation has relocated me three times now. Why? I can't remember. That's a lot of moving in eight months . . . and a lot of time spent alone. Equivalent to a year-and-a-half on Mares, I've experienced most of my teenage levels and early twenties: alone.

I remember Ariyan going off for training right after our guardians were sent away. I was level twelve when their MAD mission was scheduled for one month, which turned to three, and then five. Now, we're not given updates. I don't know who was more shocked that they were still gone after Ariyan returned from Zero Zone 2034; me or him. They're still gone, and Ariyan's due to depart again. Oh, I want to go with Ariyan so bad. My allevelations seem to happen more rapidly the longer I am on Arth; and the more educated I become, the more deprived I feel from what I desire.

I desire freedom outside of these silo walls. My inner intelligence finally chimes in, **_"Come back to your mission."_** *CLICK*. That's right! I get permitted to go with Ariyan this time. *SNAP*. Strange . . . I know it, yet, I still feel sadness. *CLICK*. I know why . . .

It's not just leaving here; it's wanting to feel whole. The UN should keep their word, and let our duality guardians return to us. I love being given substitute guardians knowing damn well that these host prana constitute as _artificial intelligence_ in comparison to the caliber of lave I understand. The UN is sadly mistaken if they think they are fooling me. I have a very bitter taste toward this never-ending MAD mission of theirs. I want my whole clan, and my version of a normal life. Wait, what is my normal? I focus on this memory and I take a deep breath. I begin to ponder, knowing that I am here for a reason.

Ariyan brings me back, "You won't be here much longer, Susun. Almost home." He shoots me another burst of hope. We hope that this news of my allevelation reunites our clan. Oh, how I yearn to know their return date. We'll be home in no time.

Staring at the house in front of me, my hope shifts back to my conversation with Commander: "I would be neglecting you by having you remain in this commune." Why did he say that? I begin to feel uneasy. I lift my left hand up, making sure I'm still solid, as Ariyan turns toward me, derailing my train of thought as he embraces my hand. I turn to him and crash into such doting eyes.

He lets out a wondrous, "Wow." In a flash, I see Cassiopeia's twinkle in his eyes; he says, "Arth will never be the same." He motions that he is ready to exit the hovercraft. I follow his lead. He waits for me to get around to his side, before we walk to the front door.

Ariyan out-etiquettes me by holding open the door. I curtsey and take the lead. We walk into our host parents sitting down for their afternoon tea and curry time. With four places set, it appears as though they've waited for us. Before Amelia even opens her mouth, I am flooded by endless passive-aggressive flashbacks I have become accustomed to with her. It is reinforced by her drawled-out apology, "Well, I am ever so sorry I did not predict that y'all would be tardy once again. Bet'cha knew we'd be waiting here though. Y'all just make a habit for all this curry to just sit here, becoming cold, like our once piping-hot tea."

Amelia never ceases to amaze me. I almost feel bad, until I see the beads of sweat on their foreheads. Who eats boiling hot food on boiling hot days? We really did them a favor. Yes, they were waiting for a good amount of time, but they had to wait anyway.

Typical Amelia. Always trying to double down on her guilt trip. She sounds foolish. I bite my tongue from almost retorting, "Oh, sorry, Mel. I know how much you love waiting on us ungrateful aliens." This situation was perfectly justified for using "Minnesota Nice"; I just cannot bring myself to utter sarcasm out loud.

Before they get another word out, Ariyan delivers a sincere apology, "Please. Please forgive us for our delay, Braxton and Amelia. We were just caught up in history being written! My baby sister, Susun, has just become the youngest Maresan—nay, the youngest being—to accomplish a complete vessel projection!"

Braxton looks at both of us and rolls his eyes. "What are you going on about? You don't have to make up excuses. Just wash up and get ready to eat." Ariyan makes haste to dart into the kitchen to wash his hands. I look at my hands and decide they are clean enough. I approach the farthest place setting. Ariyan boasts loudly, "You should have seen her projection! I didn't even know what was going on when the squirrel popped up on its two hind legs, but I was up for anything after discovering Susun can read auras."

As I take a seat, I smile at the observation of steam still rising from the curry. This is short-lived. At almost the same time, a rising feeling informs me that I shouldn't be here. Ariyan is still in the kitchen, so he does not see what I do. Amelia and Braxton are in disbelief, nervously laughing a bit, before they start making subtle yet unmistakable head gestures at one another.

Amelia goes from playing fake nice to one of those faces we pass by in the commune. She looks at me in a way I soon hope to forget. Her eyes, usually full of fluorescent light, are tinted over with a dimmed look of: MENACE. VACANCY TERMINATED. She doesn't excuse herself, just dashes off into the study. I hear her use the phone. Ariyan finally joins us at the table, while Braxton starts to serve himself some curry. I can tell that Ariyan is not picking up the same reading as me. He seems clueless to the tension even after Braxton slams down the serving bowl.

"The fact is, what Susun claims to have experienced is not possible. Ariyan, have you ever heard the phrase"—Braxton uses air quotes—"she's faking it?" Braxton's mannerisms perturb me. Who does he think he is to deny something I did? On what grounds? And such a perverted way to belittle my accomplishment. Again, I will never use those quotes, and neither should he. Ariyan innocently shakes his head no.

I lean forward to shed some enlightenment, "Actually Braxton, I did in fact access—"

My words must have instilled fear into Braxton, who now raises his voice. "How dare you challenge my knowledge of—you're lying! How dare you lie in my house! Everyone knows it takes at least thirty levels before aura reading can be accomplished."

I smirk, and correct him, "Actually, Braxton. The earliest was level thirty-one; before today. And that's—"

Braxton works himself into a panic. "I'm—I'm gonna' write you up, and you . . ."

Braxton spouts off nonsense as Ariyan advises me, *"Sonder, now might not be the time to correct a hueman being who is super defensive. He's not thinking clearly. Remember the convenience store owner?"*

I don't know what he's referring to, but calmly respond, *"But Yan, he's only defensive because he's protecting a falsehood. I know he'll calm down once he is reminded that this is programmed in his conditioning—"*

Braxton goes ballistic. "Hey! Stop talking about me inside your heads, you little freaks! That's all you do! That's all you two ever do is spread lies, lies, li—"

Out of nowhere, Braxton stands up and lunges at me. I turn away and am shielded as Ariyan stands in front of me, blocking him. "I order you to step down, Mr. Bivit. It's factual, Susun Forkins was able to aura read, and while vessel projecting, she communicated to me through the squirrel. I will vouch for her against any—"

Braxton hisses, "Oh!" He shrivels back to his place setting. "Amelia! Amelia, come quick! He—he was going to hit me! They are out to get us, for—for catching them in this lie!" Catch us? What, wait?

I seek clarification. "Braxton, are you mad?" He slams the table with both hands, as if he's solved the riddle. "What a bastardized story, you bastards have told! I figured it out. Adrian told Susun how to engage in aura reading, and connect to sleepers, and now you were planning to beat me up for turning them in! He dishonored the oath—and I caught them in the act! He's to blame for corruption in this world, the lack of integrity of honoring our world of words! I figured it out!"

Ariyan reacts. "No! We didn't! I can't even do a vessel projection! She did it . . . I didn't—I obeyed! I obeyed! I—"

Braxton snickers, "Why aren't you calm now?"

Amelia returns, "Prepare your things. You two may no longer stay here. We are kicking you out."

Braxton becomes so enlivened by this news, it is almost unbearable. He truly is mad. I turn on my aura reader, and realize that Braxton is merlot red—he's just not willing to connect. I turn to relay this information to Ariyan, who isn't much better. He's currently at a garnet red; I almost jump, but try to bury this bewilderment. I nonchalantly turn to Ariyan. "Hey, Adrian, let's go pack up our things, okay. This is no big deal; let's not get worked up about it. Almost home."

Ariyan grinds his teeth. *You tricked me. How dare you use me . . . Curse you, Sonder Light. I swear to the ends of life, lave, and this universe, I will expose your deceitful ways. You have dishonored our guardians—and me with your lies.*

I'm in disbelief. *"Oh, come on. You know this isn't true! I didn't use anyone. I'm just learning really quickly."*

He is stone cold toward me. I leap out of my chair in a panic. "Adrian, you know me . . . Wait, you believe me, right? Hey, I'm not lying—snap out of it! Yan? Adrian!"

His face hardens; I tele, *"Ariyan, whatever is the matter?"*

No acknowledgment. He looks at the table, and then takes his seat again. "You go pack first; I will pack my things once you're done."

Braxton looks at me with eager eyes and anticipates—or at least hopes for me to break. With Ariyan staring ahead blankly, I push in the chair, knowing I will never use it again. My head directs me to leave, but my heart cannot without one final plea. "Please, look at me." And another. "Please, Adrian! Your aura is red; please connect with me! You said you'd never leave me for too long. Please connect, Adrian?"

I hold up my palm to him. "You promised! You never promise, but you promised!"

Ariyan laces his fingers and turns ever-so obediently to Braxton, "No promises." Braxton takes his seat and begins eating, as if nothing happened. I watch as Amelia dramatically dashes out of the other room. She makes it clear she wants nothing to do with us as she closes the door. I look at Braxton, who gestures for me to join them at the table. I chose to remove myself from the situation. I drop my hand and turn my back to Ariyan.

I love the hueman conditioning. *SNAP*.

I head to the back room—not to pack, but to rebelliously lie on the floor. I stare up at the ceiling as I walk through the draped curtain. It hits me that I will be visited by Commander today. I look back at the draped curtain, and I realize I would be leaving this house whether I go with him or not. If I were to stay on Arth, I would begin a new loop with another host family. Fourth time's the charm, I suppose. I cannot remember if the previous two host clans resulted like this. Why is this so difficult? *SNAP*.

I activate the ceiling fan, find my spot in the center of the room on my circular rug, and then dramatically drop my back and throw my arms behind me. So this is restarting the silo loop; back in the null space of my hueman experience. It does not seem to matter which silo I'm in, I seem to branch out probably in a similar fashion, expanding in the same direction, with the same results; relocation. Oh, I want to go home. *CLICK*. Now I know why I was crying.

I dash the false hopes of my guardians coming to get us . . . Commander ends up coming, and then I'm whisked away to Zero Zone. When do I see them again? My heart breaks over and over again. This universe is cruel. I have no idea what is being said to Ariyan now that I retreated from Braxton's verbal attack. I feel helpless. I don't deserve to be cast away; but I no longer wish to be here. Not much longer until Commander gets me. But when? What time is it?

I wipe my cheeks, now covered in streams of tears. Even though I know it is Commander who will come, I still wish for my guardians. Please, Allah . . . let my guardian make it back safely to Arthling rock. Please; please, Allah.

Once the chatter dies down, I hear two sets of feet make haste to join me in the backroom; Ariyan is not present. The Bivits stand above me and ask if everything is okay—as if nothing has happened. I say nothing. How could they be so oblivious to the damage they inflicted on me? Parents of this planet are so pretentious. It really grosses me out how they have been conditioned to try to maintain falsified personas, choosing to abandon responsibility for their words and actions earlier. I tune out for the majority of what they squeak. I only hear that Apollo and Cassiopeia will not be able to make it.

They happily inform me that it might be another Arth year or two before they return, and that I should be grateful to know I've been reassigned to the silo. I know I won't make it in another silo—I need out. I'm craving praise after being rejected, yearning greatly and wanting lave. Lave and answers! I need answers. Why was I able to read auras before I was supposed to? Even if I knew about it, how was I able to do a vessel projection? Why was I able to access this ability prematurely? And why did those memories come back to me in reverse order? Oh, what are the answers—oh, the answers I long for!

This memory was supposed to give me reassurance to what I did not know, not add more convolution and anxiety. I look into the deadened eyes of both Amelia and Braxton, hoping for them to fill me with a bit of balance in lave, life, and the universe. I cannot hear their words over my heart pounding in my head. With clarity, I finally hear my inner voice. ***"Silly Sonder. Change your position on this truth. Focus, Sonder. Focus. Just because others are creating limitations, don't forget you are limitless! You are discovering it in divine order. Everything happens with absolute divinity . . ."*** *CLICK*. That is the truth—my truth. It might be different from theirs, and both are valid in our different universes.

I close my eyes and focus on a new game. My game is restoring balance in lave, life, and my universe. I genuinely smile. Now, my ex-host clan exit through the draped doorway. I feel it; I will never see them again. Impulsively I shout out, "I lave you two." I mean it. They say nothing in return; it does not alter my experience, or the true intent behind my words. I know I lave them, regardless of if they are incapable of lave. I wish them well in their game of perpetual catch twenty-two. I have a feeling they might be going for another round on this level. As for me, I think I'm breaking out. I hold up my right and then left hand; both illuminate violet auras. I understand what I'm experiencing: the feeling of being forced to leave.

The feeling is similar to having my duality guardians removed from my life with no say on my side. It alters one's mentality. A forced detachment has the same emotional indicator that one might experience at death. To never see another again. Most who feel great loss have been conditioned to hold resentment and sorrow. I was taught that loss is a beautiful thing—if you are willing to explore it.

Cassiopeia's voice drifts back to me. "Because once you discover that you cannot lose anything that is truly yours, you are free once more. You are free to return to lave, then happiness."

7 WAR WITHIN WORLDS

FLASH. I return back to my resting unit with so many questions. I know I ended up going to Spacer University with Commander, but I still do not know why Cassiopeia and Apollo never answered our calls. Who did Amelia call? Did she call Commander? Why wouldn't Ariyan connect with me, or believe me? Oh, answers! I need answers!

CLICK. Maybe I can ask Commander where our guardians went. He has to know.

Quickly, I lay still, trying to return to the memory of his visit. I begin to envision his sweaty uniform . . . nothing. I think about his matching hat . . . nothing. I try to feel that circular rug beneath me; still nothing. Drats! How can I get back there? *CLICK*. MIT! There's no time to lose, I look back on my entries. Frantically I scan the pages sure to find one with Commander's name that I can—oh! Magically, one face jumps into my head: Cassiopeia. She seems to be sitting on the floor. I draw nearer to her. I seem to be crawling toward her. Everything, besides her face, goes black.

FLASH. I hear a giggle, then I'm lifted up by a tiny pair of hands; I know it's Ariyan. He walks with me dangling from his arms to Cassiopeia.

Cassiopeia wears an attentive face as she reminds him, "Gentle with your sibling, Yanny." Suddenly the room begins to whirl, and the lights illuminate the room.

Trying to not step on my tentacles, Ariyan assures Cassiopeia, "I know, I know. I won't hurt her. Because I lave her. I lave you, Sonder. Very much."

His response makes Cassiopeia's face shift with delight. "Ah. That's what I like to hear—acts of lave." Ariyan plops me down within a tentacle's reach of Cassiopeia's knee. My yin shares a jovial smile with me.

"That's the thing about lave," Cassiopeia explains, "and everything that's part of the universal cycle. It burns brightly and unapologetically, from degeneration to regeneration. The flowing cycle continuously repeats, altering minute bits of history to make it unique for all versions of existence. The experience of lave manifests a deep understanding of mentally committing oneself. It can align one's mental and spiritual experience of happiness, through trust and affinity, if they can go beyond miscommunications and conditioned beliefs."

A few of Cassiopeia's golden curls cascade forward and my instincts kick in to reach out to touch some of the loose strands of hair. They cascade effortlessly as she leans into me, so I can easily touch her luscious locks, and whispers, "Be gentle, my little one." She reaches up with her right hand to

149

demonstrate. "Like this." She twirls a little ringlet, and it springs back.

I giggle with delight—I think back now; I must be level two during this memory. I look at Ariyan's Arthling skin suit—probably level seven or eight, wearing a face of sadness. I draw attention to him as I tele, *"Yan?"*

Cassiopeia uses her left hand to softly bring up his chin. "Why, whatever is the matter, my little prince?"

Ariyan, almost in tears, responds, "How come my dare don't curl dup?"

Cassiopeia moves both hands to the top of his crown. "Yanny, your HAIR DOES NOT curl UP, because in this wonderful universe, you were gifted blond hair that goes straight down." She tousles his hair. "Color from me, consistency from Apollo. You are the duality of Apollo and me."

Ariyan sits up proudly and then cuts into laughter as she tickles him. She looks over at me. "And for my little squishy sunspot . . ." She gets high on her knees. "Can you say your sibling's name?"

I quickly tele, *"Ariyan! His name is Ariyan!"*

Now Ariyan has recovered. "Say it loudly . . ." They both look ready to attack me.

I take a big gulp and shout, "Yan! Is name is A-yan!"

Cheers burst out as she scoops me up, and rocks me. "Yay, yay! You said it, Sonny-girl!" I get numerous kisses, and when I'm put back down, Ariyan kisses my forehead.

150

I am wildly blessed to be formed through Apollo and Cassiopeia. My clan is built on the ultimate triforce of lave. The lave to pursue happiness, trust, and affinity within this universe. Cassiopeia explains, "The key in discovering lave is first discovering one's own happiness. How can one find happiness with another, if one does not first know happiness with one's self?" Both Ariyan and I shake our heads with uncertainty.

Cassiopeia continues, "The importance of happiness was overlooked eons ago. Even with guidance from Sir Reginald and Andromeda that highlighted the need to take hold of our responsibility for individual happiness, it seems it was still cast in the shadow of the lave story."

Ariyan teles, *"I thought Sir Reginald was only a lave story. Is it really about being responsible for our own happiness?"*

Cassiopeia nods. "It is both; and the reason it is brilliant is that it demonstrates the sacrifice lave is willing to make to put happiness first."

Satisfied with this, Ariyan leans forward as she continues, "During the War within Worlds, most didn't understand this, and there were unnecessary lives lost due to this misunderstanding. Most battles were justified in order to protect the lives of laved ones, but how can that be justice if life on the other side thinks the same way?" Ariyan and I shake our heads. We do not have an answer.

Cassiopeia concludes, "Justice is not a solution. Mercy is. We always suffer loss of Self when we harm each other. That's why Apollo and I choose to support happiness. There is no harm to be had if we truly pursue our own happiness."

I chime in, "Why?"

She responds, "Because, when pursuing true happiness, you will feel it instantly when your actions hurt another. When pain is inflicted, happiness doesn't exist. Many prana in war feel this, this convicted, 'us versus them,' manipulated mentality. Then they return to their home planet conflicted after battle—if they return."

I cling to Cassiopeia's words as she continues. "The time I speak of predates the word lave. The time when planets invaded planets; it was an era of Wars within Worlds. Galaxies versus galaxies. It was nonsensical; and the worst was between Regins and Andromedans. Before lave, there was a constant misunderstanding of what lava and leve meant, what I call the War with Words. In some galaxies, it was just a pronunciation disagreement; but between the Regins and Andromedans, leve and lava were fighting words. Lave only happened because two starlights from these two different galaxies wanted to understand one another. Only then did the words lava and leve alter—"

Ariyan blurts out, "That's you and Apollo!"

I swivel to Ariyan and back to a blushing Cassiopeia. "It seems it is always easier to predict history once it's happened. Yes, but in this part of the story we did not know our role in universal history, or for each other, or that there was going to be a day that ended the Wars within Worlds."

Cassiopeia looks into both our eyes. "I still remember . . . watching the shadow grow darker." Her eyes fill with wonder, and then confusion, "I was just level eighteen when the hollow-looking cloud slowly hovered down from the outer atmosphere. It blocked the whole tyrian sky, and not knowing what it was, I wanted to see if it stretched beyond my sleepy little valley. I jet-setted up, quickly wriggling myself to the top of the hill to observe its beauty. I ended up on the highest hill with the best view of my little village, called Chivalry. It was almost noon, so when I reached the bottom of the hills, I headed up the one containing a tiny forest of tall willowy trees to serve as a shaded barrier as I peered over my valley; I'd never seen Chivalry from above. I could make out all our landmarks—especially the Hospitality Center that served as my home with my eight laved ones. I was so foolish to marvel at this dark, translucent haze with a heart full of admiration."

Cassiopeia returns to that moment—just as she reached the top of the hill and tried to catch her breath. A moment of naive bliss; not knowing what was to come. Cassiopeia licked her lips, "Right before I reach the top of the hill, I look outward onto this unknown cast shadow whirling above. It began receding and condensing, and concentrating above my Hospitality Center's rooftop. All I thought, the one thing I wished into the looming cloud, before it altered my world: 'I wish my clan was here to see this.'"

Cassiopeia reports in a state of solitude. "I remember the feeling, wanting my whole life to see

Allah, and at that moment thinking I was watching him take his truest and most pure form in a cloud to pour down in a beautiful shower of lave. While only thinking beautiful thoughts, I would soon become the witness to an act of diabolical destruction."

FLASH. It's as if I am there, on that hill. I watch Cassiopeia relive her sequence precisely. The swirling cloud contracts into a tiny sphere. Sporadically, it changes through multiple different color hues. It condenses so much; it appears to vanish as if nothing further will happen. Then . . . blip! A radiant shimmer of light, no bigger than a freckle, begins dropping down onto the roof of the Hospitality Center, which protected all of her laved ones. The moment it touches, a *FLASH* brighter than a lit magnesium strip goes off. A glint flickers in her eyes, before she closes them tightly. Instantly she knows she won't be seeing her clan again. Ash ripples out and consumes the valley. Helplessly, she watches a tsunami of dirt and hears frantic screams, followed by complete silence.

The smell of wood burning is nauseating, and causes her to recoil and retract her tentacles. Tears stream from Cassiopeia's sealed eyes. As if she forgot to breathe, she collapses on the hill and gasps for air. The only part of the universe she knew is now flattened. The only place in her world she knew; erased. The prana she knew or laved; gone. These lush green hills; barren. Apart from the tips of higher peaks, her valley looks like a rust-ringed bathtub; everything below the line was now washed down its dismal drain.

Cassiopeia wears a half-hysterical smile, thinking ironically of her Yin-Yin teasing her. She used to say, 'Honestly, Cassiopeia, there's more to life than working to serve others. Just watch—one day you'll head for the hills and never return.' Her Yin-Yin always had magic words; if only her magic spells were reversible. Cassiopeia wanted to prove her wrong.

Cassiopeia lies on her back, hugging herself, clinging to her belief that Allah will reverse it. "I wish today was not the day I stepped outside of my center. I wish to return to my home. I wish for my clan to be up here with me. Please bring them back! Please!"

Several moments pass, and then the narrative shifts. "Curse you, Allah! You let this happen. You are a tyrant! I will never serve you again!" She finally collects herself enough and begins staring up into the trees. Staring into the branches, she asks the leaves, "Why me? Why today? If this took place any other day, yesterday or tomorrow, I might not have even taken the time to look up at the sky. Why did they send me out? Eighteen is not a big deal. Why did I agree?"

The leaves give no answer, but she does hear just what she needs. The tiniest voice begins to whisper magical words at that moment: "Everything is done with absolute divinity; If it doesn't happen, it wasn't meant to be." *CLICK*.

FLASH. I almost jump in, but Ariyan beats me to it. "Who else was there? Who whispered such profound words?"

I telepathically blurt out, *"It was her inner intelligence. Yin already had the magic words inside."*

Both of them look at me, and Cassiopeia confirms, "That was it. It was my inner intelligence chiming in. Something we all have, and can hear in moments when we align with our Self." Cassiopeia looks back and forth between the two of us. "When I sat up, scanning the few green-tipped hills, you know what I realized?" Both of us shake our heads. She continues, "I realized if I hadn't headed for the trees, I might not have survived the blast. I knew the universe forced me out of Chivalry on that day, but at the moment, I was not ready to find out why. I lay down and passed out from exhaustion."

With a sigh of what I interpret as relief, she reaches for my head. It shocks me when I feel her wrap her finger around one of my dark-brown ringlets. *CLICK*. I have my hair? I touch a head full of curly hair. I look down, and am no longer a squishy little Maresan—I am indeed back in my young Arthling form, but many levels of alevelation later; beyond two or three now!

I look over at Ariyan, who is also much further along in adolescence; perhaps fifteen or sixteen levels. Is this the same memory? Is this the same story?

Curiously, I ask, "Wad 'appened?"

Ariyan answers, "I'll tell you WHAT HAPPENED. Total mooks tried to destroy a benevolent world, but that benevolent world sacrificed its land for our yin's life. The one from Chivalry who lived! She was about to create history!"

156

Scanning the last bit of the story I remember hearing, it sounds about right. Still, I clarify, "Was she the only one found alive?"

Ariyan rolls his eyes. "Don't jump ahead in the story. Just because you know the story doesn't mean you can skip ahead . . . or try to rewrite it, as most prana do."

Okay. Same story, different time period in my memory . . . Perhaps I'm connecting like memories. I ask for clarity, "Did anyone ever figure out what led to the attacks?"

Ariyan chimes in, "No. Not much is known about the attacks that day. Many versions of truth say it was a rip in the fabric of our reality from alternate realities trying to experience their different lifetimes. Others claim it was rogue galaxies conspiring to restore fear in those who believed in mercy over justice. And there's a bogus conspiracy about the old Universal Network trying to gain support for their armed forces. Whatever your flavor, no one has ever admitted to these heinous crimes. A serious group of cowardly mooks."

Cassiopeia concludes, "Regardless of the cause, I knew I had to leave Chivalry."

8 CUSTOMER SERVICE

Cassiopeia continues the story.

FLASH. That evening, giant beams of light flood Cassiopeia's flattened world, causing her to stir awake. Frantically, she teles, *"I'm here! I'm here! On this hill; next to the trees! I'm here."* After she says this over and over again to the brink of exhaustion, the hovercraft drops down and rescues her. As she's pulled onboard, Cassiopeia collapses while saying, "Oh, Allah! Thank you. I—I don't know where to go, and—and I . . ." She faints.

Cassiopeia wakes up when the moon is high. She overhears, "That's the end of the line. At least we saved one." There's a transmission made: "We rescued one young yin from a remote village. Returning to headquarters; clear." Cassiopeia comes to terms with being the only survivor. Not wanting to distract the pilot or copilot, she directs her attention outside the window.

In solace, Cassiopeia begins to realize how much of her world she missed while living solely in

Chivalry. Geographically, the village of Chivalry was a pond compared to the great lakes she flies over. Tragically, three major cities she hovers over are no more than massive rings of fire. Every valley and open field she passes no longer seems functional. These cities dwarf her village in comparison, but now are all similar in their silence.

As they approach the highest mountain range in the governing city of Mares, her inner intelligence reminds her through Andromeda's jingle, " . . . You might say you wanna stay here forever, but it is worth it to let go -n- explore!" She isn't going home, but she feels safe going. She feels an urge to remember she was put on that hill to survive; she doesn't know why, but she trusts she'll discover it soon enough.

The hovercraft returns to the landing docks at Universal Networks Headquarters. When Cassiopeia lands, she is brought into Universal Network's Main Hall of History to meet Ariyan. Ariyan is the Peace Marshal for the Maresan Peace Department. The moment Ariyan sees Cassiopeia, he lights up and declares, "Even though it's our first time meeting—I already knew you were coming. It's as if I expected it."

It's an odd way to greet someone, causing Cassiopeia to become defensive, "Sir, I had no intention of leaving Chivalry today . . . I never intended on leaving my village ever. This has been quite an experience, and I do not know where I fit in outside of my valley."

With a look of clear understanding, he says, "Ah. Seems like a reasonable and very normal curiosity . . . I assure you. Well then! We shall figure it out together. Today, we've all experienced great loss. My clan of six is down to two. My offspring Omega and I are coping very differently."

Cassiopeia drops her guard, "Oh! I'm so sorry. I had no idea, Sir. I—"

"Call me Ariyan," Ariyan interjects. "And let's talk over dinner; I'm famished. Are you hungry?" Cassiopeia nods meekly, knowing she hasn't eaten all day. Not wanting to intrude, she asks, "May I prepare it?"

Ecstatically, Ariyan accepts, "Oh, absolutely! With everything that happened today, the staff was dismissed; but between us two, I think we could find our way around that kitchen. Shall we?"
Cassiopeia and Ariyan both find themselves making their way through the kitchen effortlessly; Cassiopeia gets the layout much quicker. She inquires, "Will there be more joining us, or just us?"

Ariyan thinks, "Perhaps Omega, my eldest offspring. I haven't a clue where he went off to . . . I'll also ask the search team to see how many are still on-duty." In total, Cassiopeia prepares enough for two dozen prana—more than enough.

Astonished, Ariyan asks, "You certainly know your way around this large kitchen. Do you make large meals like this often?"

"Yes. Twice a day; I have . . . well, had six younger yang siblings and my duality guardians to cook for; and we'd usually have a dozen or so guests with us at a time."

Ariyan nods. "I see. Did you often have visiting guests outside of your clan?"

"Yes. My clan ran the Chivalry Hospitality Center in our village. Oftentimes, my siblings would try to help in the kitchen; but I'd send them away to clean our daily guests' rooms. In exchange, I'd cook all the meals and clean up afterward. The nine of us ran the finest Hospitality Center. We are world-renowned; known by all the other centers. Sure we had our struggles, but always handled all squabbles with leve and kindness . . . we had a working system; truly a clan-run business."

Elated, Ariyan tries to relate. "Huzzah! I've never heard of a Hospitality Center, but that's our vision too for the Universal Network—well, my vision. I always wanted a working environment that acts and treats fellow workers as their own clan. My partner and offspring don't—errr . . . didn't share the same desires for work—errr . . . in our home either. Never wanting to work, but always willing to take my rewards. They love living on this mountain and using my established credibility and reputation in the community . . . well, they did, but they never listened to me. I wish—I wish I would have tried harder to keep them here today." He falls silent. Cassiopeia doesn't know what to do, so she keeps preparing the food.

Several moments pass before Ariyan jumps back in. "Enough about me . . . What about your life? I'm ashamed to say, I've never heard of Chivalry. What was it like?"

The question seems to bring Cassiopeia alive, as if asked to put on a show. She begins stringing together memories of her village, "Chivalry was remarkable; even if it was your first time navigating those city streets, they generously propelled you over their worn cobblestones, down the most lively alleyways, always leading with this lingering sense of nostalgia. Leaving my center today felt like stepping away from the mundane and into a world of magic! Staring up at our tyrian sky with fresh eyes was like seeing the play of a memorized manuscript. With much wonder, I left as my clan waved me off. Their giddiness and immeasurable excitement for me to leave were matched by their anticipation for me to return. They knew I'd bring back vibrant stories of my adventure."

Cassiopeia starts mixing the food while continuing to speak. "Chivalry has no strangers; everyone is familiar. You see yourself in everyone you cross paths with. You feel it over and over again, as it effortlessly guides you through the bustling crowds, right where you're supposed to be. All the songs are known by heart, and its rich aromas do not seem to end. At all hours of the day, the tunes will chime with cheer and glee, while the sweet scents of bread will waft endlessly. Oh! And the colors! Never have you seen such pinks, yellows and unnatural-looking blues."

Cassiopeia's eyes begin to scintillate. "Honest to Allah, I didn't even know teal or aqua existed until today."

"Today," Ariyan follows up, "was it different from yesterday, or the day before?"

Cassiopeia shakes her head, "I . . . I don't actually know. Today was the first time I ever left my Hospitality Center since I was level one."

Ariyan is astonished. "My word! How did you—didn't your guardians let you out?"

Cassiopeia shrugs. "I always declined. I saw no need. I had everything I ever wanted there. My clan, my comforts, my work . . . my world. I only agreed to go out today, because . . . I turned level eighteen. I chose a confusing day to allevelate and discover beauty."

Dumbfounded, Ariyan clarifies, "Your description of your town was from one day?" She nods.

"From one time out?" She nods.

"And that one day happened to be today?" She nods.

"And you just turned level eighteen after discovering beauty?"

She nods and adds, "And for what it's worth, I did discover beauty today—in everything that Allah has given to me. And now I know not to leve anything, because when he takes it . . . it only leads to destruction. I just wish . . . I wish I hadn't said yes to leaving today . . . Life was simpler inside of my center."

Ariyan becomes uneasy with Cassiopeia's words. "My dear, surely you don't mean that. I mean, if you'd stayed in your center, you would not have survived." She does not answer, continuing to combine ingredients. Ariyan, still uneasy, chooses to sit with his feelings for a while longer.

Ariyan collects himself enough to focus back as Cassiopeia starts cooking the food. "This is a lot to unpack, and frankly, I do not know how you are so composed. Okay, what would you feel comfortable doing about living arrangements? Do you have any distant clan members that you know of?" Cassiopeia does not answer; she just shakes her head. There were none that she knew; and even if she did, what were the chances that they survived?

Ariyan makes an offer. "You may stay in my home for as long as you need to recover. I have more than enough room, and it's—"

Cassiopeia stops preparing and interrupts him. "Oh, Sir, I couldn't poss—"

Ariyan cuts her off. "Please accept this generosity. And it comes without any urgency to return to the working world. As it is, by preparing this single elaborate meal, you're working more than my whole clan ever did. I insist. Honestly, I feel I'm doing this more for me than you. Your presence is needed here; you have the nerves of a goddess. Trust me."

Nothing he says fazes her. He asks, "How are you so calm, and without a trace of desperation to be shown?"

Cassiopeia automatically responds, "That answer is simple; I have no choice." Cassiopeia studies Ariyan's face. He is in awe of her. She purses her lips. "I will accept your offer of hosting me, if you agree to two things: one, we share dinners together. And two, you never assume an answer I might give without asking me first. Deal?"

"Deal."

They shake tentacles and continue preparing dinner. Not another word is spoken about their pasts.

The rescue team dinner begins with the end-of-day shift report, which is bleak considering the events of the day. A shared moment of silence was followed by many cherished memories in their destroyed cities. It was a true loss of worlds, and now the staff feels a new low in hope. It isn't until the rich fragrances of the flavor-filled dishes fill the room that it's brought back to life. All attention is on Cassiopeia as she introduces herself and announces that dinner is ready. Each platter presented to the team seems to be crafted to nourish the depleted morale.

During dinner, Ariyan asks Cassiopeia if she'll share her captivatingly vivid story of Chivalry. Not many have heard of her village, but all enjoy her story. She then shares some of her personal antics of what life is like when growing up in a small village, followed with laughter as she recalls embarrassing moments while working within hospitality.

All admire her bravery to share with them, and the comedic relief keeps coming when the search team begins sharing their off-the-clock personal moments. For the first time, many of these staff members are sharing in ways they never thought possible among one another. Laughter fills the air as the sorrows of the days end. With gratitude, they realize that there is still life to be lived, and laughter to be shared.

It all remains very light-hearted and jovial until Omega emerges from his solitude. "Yangs! What's going on here? This doesn't seem typical of y'all serious staff meetings. If I'd known it'd be a par-tay, I would have drunk my bottle with y'all instead—" He makes eyes at Cassiopeia. "Well, hello, gorgeous!"

"Omega, don't be rude," Ariyan interrupts. "This is Cassiopeia. She comes from a village that . . . has been completely destroyed."

Cassiopeia nods. "Yes. I survived the blast while on top of a hill. The cloud dropped down and flattened—"

"Wait. Woah, wait . . . you saw it come down from the sky? Ariyan, I thought you said it was a series of implanted detonations? Was this an aerial invasion?" All eyes go between Ariyan and Cassiopeia.

Cassiopeia looks into Ariyan's eyes. "I know what I saw . . ." She looks at everyone. "A giant cloud that loomed above my village, shrank into a little ball, and dropped down onto my beautiful Hospitality Center's rooftop."

Omega shakes his head. "I apologize for your loss. Really, baby, I am sorry. If you need a place to stay, you have a place with us." Everyone's attention is on Omega.

Ariyan begins, "Omega, Cassiopeia already—"

Omega jumps in, "Look, Ariyan . . ." He tenses up as he continues. "We have to think about her. You always talk about all prana having a purpose, and how if encouraged, they will find divinity. Well, I think it's time you support that. Cassiopeia, sweetness; it's in Ariyan's demeanor. He will never give up on others." He winks. "And that fruit doesn't fall far from the tree."

Cassiopeia purses her lips, "I accept the offer. And having no doubt in Ariyan's character, I—"

Omega cuts her off, "Well, if you like that offer, I've got another one I'd like to run by you later." He winks, causing Ariyan to step in. "That will be quite enough, Omega. There will be no more offers made this evening. And Cassiopeia, this might be a lot to take in, but . . . you might be the only witness still alive. We can discuss this tomorrow. Do you need anything right now?"

All are quiet; no one moves.

Cassiopeia looks directly at Omega as if in a trance. "Purpose. I need a purpose in my life right now."

Omega arrogantly states, "Well, well, well! If you're looking for your purpose, you've found the best at long last."

Someone whispers, "Mook."

Omega hisses, "Who said that?" Then he looks back at Cassiopeia with a genuine smile.

Cassiopeia returns to full alert; her attention has targeted Ariyan. "I wish to be of service and do what I can to encourage others to pursue their purposes. I might have lost my home, but I did not lose my heart; I wish to aid those who are still with us. I saw what I saw, I survived for a reason, and I will not rest until I know why I did not perish like my leved ones."

Omega starts it, but soon everyone joins in on the round of applause.

FLASH. Cassiopeia looks at both Ariyan and me. "It was that single conversation that gave us the missing piece. The next morning, we discovered that only hospitality centers had been attacked; no one knew why. What happened in Chivalry simultaneously happened on all known planets with centers. The art of hospitality would've been lost if I hadn't been on that hill. I alone carried this craft. Everyone at dinner shared how enlivened they felt. Hospitality began infusing the Universal Network, and within one moon cycle, I was given my own office! Ariyan was put in charge of my affairs, which worked out magically."

Cassiopeia sheepishly admits, "Little did I know how misunderstood hospitality was. It only became clear when I saw the words engraved above my office: Customer Service."

From behind me, I hear Apollo chuckling. "Explaining the differences between servants and those of service, are we?"

Cassiopeia rolls her eyes a bit. "Not outright. The story does what it does."

Apollo crouches down by Ariyan and explains, "Well, it's important to recognize when misinformation transpires into neglecting Self-care. You might be able to handle it, but is it worth the cost of breaking your own rules?"

Cassiopeia scoffs. "I have risen beyond my hypocrisy, mister."

Apollo agrees, "Yes, but you no longer had humble guests, just demanding customers; a bit different, no?"

Cassiopeia admits, "Yes, at first—but it was still manageable. I provided hospitality for all who came into my office. The results were always satisfactory . . . even though my devotion to my craft left me exhausted. They'd come to me with life problems, and demand attention immediately. It was like being considered a doctor that cured illnesses they'd had for decades, always expected to provide solutions on the same day of their visit. They believed my universe existed to serve them. I would do what I could, with whatever window of time I was given; some were easier than others. They came from all planets and galaxies; and their situations always seemed to escalate. I was used to guests yearning to be served in the shadows back in Chivalry; now I had customers wanting to be served in the limelight. Feeling depleted and misunderstood, I almost wanted to close my doors."

Ariyan asks, "Did you ever deny anyone who asked too much of you?"

Apollo giggles and cuts in, "No one was too much for Cassiopeia."

Cassiopeia nods. "Affirmative. I trust the universe to only give me what it knows I can handle. I took everyone who desired to follow their heart. Then my skill of grace kicked in. It was more than just being hospitable; there was an art to being of service. This was not a time for me to fight flow. This was a time to flow with floricity; to live life with the least resistance. My customers wanted solutions to problems I didn't even know existed, but it didn't matter. The problems were distractions, and the solutions were easy, once I answered the question: Are they ready to listen to their heart or not?"

Cassiopeia humbly adds, "With enough mastery, while treating everyone the same, I went from providing the answers to having customers generating their own solutions. Their glowing aspirations led to dozens of new Customer Service branches opening around the universe. Allah, I was busy . . . I don't even remember having any spare time to do, or think about, anything else."

Apollo chimes in, "Busy might be true . . . Hey, weren't you also avoiding someone? Wasn't this around the time you'd received the sixth invitation for life in matrimony with Omega?"

Cassiopeia clarifies, "No! He . . . he only proposed four times."

Apollo dramatically throws his back to the floor; Ariyan and I start giggling. Cassiopeia elaborates, "I didn't leve him, and I was much too busy aligning with my purpose. Matrimony seemed too monotonous to be explored at that stage."

Apollo lifts himself up on his shoulders. "I guess that's leve for you. Just distant channels; barely keeping y'all a float."

Cassiopeia scoffs, "Really, Apollo? You're still pretending to only know your old side of the story, and not what leve meant on my side?" Apollo slyly motions with his fingers, a gesture of sealing his lips.

Cassiopeia continues, "I dreamed of experiencing such a doting leve of my own—like my guardians had when they were together. They flowed with tranquility, never turbulence. Their leve pooled so deep, never experiencing a drought. They were my idols; after losing everything in Chivalry, I no longer believed it possible to find a leve such as theirs, but I entrusted my heart to flow where it felt free. It wasn't just going to wait for someone to become whole. I had grown to leve myself. And once I did, I expanded."

Cassiopeia provides context. "Before the word lave was spoken, prana of the Reginald galaxy spoke of leve."

Apollo sits back up, and adds, "And the Andromeda galaxy spoke of lava. Regardless of the syntax used, it is clear these two starbits demonstrated unconditional acts of devotion toward one another . . . yet their ancestral stardust hadn't agreed what to call it."

I ask, "Why?"

Apollo maneuvers himself and now looks at Ariyan and me. Sitting beside Cassiopeia, he answers, "Well, Sonny-girl . . . The Andoremedans didn't want to calm down their passionate ways to please the passively placid Regins."

Cassiopeia cuts him off, "Hey!" They both stick their tongues out at each other and then start laughing. Apollo and Cassiopeia stare deeply into each other's eyes. Cassiopeia whimsically starts back in, "I remember when you first spoke the word lave. It took me by surprise."

Apollo nonchalantly turns toward Ariyan and me. "I was the one who made the word up."

Cassiopeia gasps, "Pish-posh! You did not!"

Apollo chuckles. "Okay, then what did I do?"

Cassiopeia lists it out, "Well, you took our two opposing words . . . brought awareness to their similarities, belted it out into the world, and . . . well . . ."

171

Cassiopeia looks up at the ceiling, as Apollo nudges her. "And?"

She looks back at him, "Oh, all right. You made it up."

Apollo wraps his arms around her. "I had to! No other existing word described the way I felt about the most magical Maresan! I had to redefine my words to finally see your world!" She starts to giggle, and he concludes, "Besides, when I confessed my lava first, you called me a barbaric animmel from an archaic galaxy."

Cassiopeia retorts, "Yeah, after you basically said you loved me to my face!"

Both Ariyan and I look at one another in shock. Apollo adds, "Oh! So you're still sticking with that, eh?" Apollo begins tickling Cassiopeia, who starts squirming.

Ariyan asks, "Apollo, how could you say such a thing to Cassiopeia. Love? Really? I thought you always laved our yin."

Both Cassiopeia and Apollo stop messing around, and Apollo explains, "I do. Always have. And that's the great thing about lave. It only came to be because we laved each other so much, we evolved beyond misunderstood words that distorted our worlds."

Cassiopeia puts her hand on Apollo's chest indicating she will continue, "See, our galaxies conditioned us to be repulsed by each other's acts of unconditional devotion."

Apollo claims, "I was raised with lava being your lave, and leve like love."

172

Cassiopeia says, "My leve was equivalent to lave, and lava was love. Ironically, this made the Sir Reginald story the biggest controversy known to universal language for eons. And that's how it could have kept going, because no one really wanted to understand why the other galaxy chose to live such . . . laveless lives."

Cassiopeia draws us in. "That was true while the planets were dealing with external wars. After the attack on the Hospitality Centers, all planets impacted laid down their weapons and permanently ceased from war. They took it as a sign from Allah to discontinue fighting forever. With the biggest distraction gone, it was time to mend fighting words. Actions spoke louder than our words, but our words were shaping our worlds."

Ariyan jumps in, "And then what happened?"

Apollo shrugs, "Well, let's not get ahead of ourselves. I still haven't even been introduced in this story." He winks and summarizes, "The way things were going, everyone wanted this newfound peace of mind. Being able to solve your own problems was trending, and everyone wanted a piece of peace. Your yin guardian is an inspirational icon. She was being drawn out of her shadows as the mastermind behind the scenes of self-reflection."

Cassiopeia shifts her gaze to Apollo. "Are you talking about yourself again?"

"Only if you are me," Apollo retorts while shooting her a smoldering look.

Blushing, Cassiopeia continues, "Once I expanded the department, I rebranded as

'Hospitality and Customer Service.' It grew in popularity as prana raved about the importance of self-care and responsibility for one's own being. Prana were shifting from looking outward for affirmation and praise, to looking inward to discover self-love and gratitude."

Apollos holds up a finger, "However, many prana were still swimming in pools of envy and self-love."

I tele, *"Why were they swimming?"*

Ariyan chimes in, "It's a figure of speech."

Cassiopeia explains, "Apollo means a bunch of prana were spreading rumors. There were those who thought I was using Ariyan and leading Omega on. It didn't bother me. Actually, I don't know if I got more customers because of rumors, or my tactful manner as others slandered my name. Regardless, my prosperity and popularity connected me with the most influential leaders and liaisons."

Apollo becomes proud. "This popularity captured my Empress Andromeda's attention who wanted to collaborate with the head Reginald Representatives in a ceremony to celebrate this new eon of peace, outside of the war. No surprise where it would be held, and which Reginald Representative would be in charge; the offer was given to Ariyan, who accepted it."

Cassiopeia chimes in, "The Universal Network was so pleased by all this talk of universal peace and unity that they held a press release, where Ariyan surprised everyone. He appointed me as the director for the Universal Network's Peace and Unity

174

Ceremony. Secretly, I knew I was going to run most of the show, but in his shadow. I felt exposed when he announced he wanted me to run it, the only way he knew I could—magically."

Cassiopeia points out, "I was pulling the ceremony together by finding prana to play each part perfectly. I had previous customers who were more than happy to assist—prestigious decorators, incredible chefs, and universally renowned entertainment icons eagerly waiting for me to ask a favor. It was a grandiose gift for everyone involved, especially Ariyan. He finally had an all-staff event with a group that embodied his clan-like atmosphere. It was then that I realized I hadn't assigned a role to any Andromedans. That's where Apollo came in."

Apollo leans in. "I received a transmitted request on behalf of the Universal Network to be the master of ceremonies."

Cassiopeia giggles, "Yes, your yang guardian was the first choice from his galactic leaders, because . . ." They both become hysterical.

Apollo finishes the thought, "My galaxy believed that I was an ideal spokesprana for advocating peace above war." My childish guardians can barely compose themselves, while Ariyan and I look at each other puzzled and shrug it off. Apollo completes his thought, "I should have known the universe had something going on when I received your transmission that I recall saying:"

Salutations Master Apollo Eirene -

On behalf of the Universal Network, your attendance is requested as the master of ceremonies at the first Peace and Unity Ceremony. It will be held in the Grand Ballroom at the Universal Network's Headquarters on Mares in the Reginald galaxy.

This is a celebration to honor and commemorate where we have come from, and where we are headed, as our universe strives for peace. With you as our ideal representative, we will accomplish extraordinary things.

The invitation list is set for guests who have demonstrated intention in being of service to this peaceful cause. All guests must meet at least one of the three requirements: Hold a progressive position in a relief department, be currently active in a relief operation, or hold a leadership role in education for discharged forces. You will discover you fit all three areas required, like most guests. I intend on having all of the biggest political officials and royal members of influence in attendance; and through your cunning words, I am

certain we will find our new direction
toward a universe of peaceful times.

Utmost respect,
Lady Cassiopeia Paizo

I respond, "That's so exciting!"

Cassiopeia confirms, "It was. Of course, Apollo saw it differently."

Apollo justified, "I did! Cassiopeia didn't know it then, so I had to let her know:"

Lady Cassiopeia Paizo -

Listen, I don't make words, I make
moves. And I call malarkey on the UN
bringing peace. By calling off all armed
forces, they've doomed us all. You are
mistaken if you think much is coming out
of this frilly show. We need to get back
to the front lines, and stop wasting time.
We need to fight for our freedom.

Besides, everyone in the Andromeda
galaxy knows if our Empress is involved,
it's just a big show for her. She says it's
for "insert cause," but it's really just an
evening of endless narcissism and
needless costumes; nothing is
accomplished besides inflating egos. I
know what I'm talking about—glitz and
gossip that your underdeveloped

177

Reginald galaxy wouldn't understand; no offense.

I know you Regins lava wasting time, but do yourself a favor and cancel this pointless party. There are much more useful things that could come out of that evening with that much leadership rather than just standing around a ballroom. Let me know when you're holding an effective meeting, not a gown-and-glamour gossip gala. Then we'll talk.

Best,
Master Apollo Eirene

Cassiopeia sheds light, "Researching Apollo, before inviting him, I knew his work was best done at ground zero. I had questioned Apollo's willingness to schmooze, which is what had me only invite guests with high merited rolls of servitude and influence; but Apollo still claimed them as too wealthy and privileged for his taste. Thankfully, I did not go in with a predisposition. Perhaps most Andromedans thought this was another frilly show, but us Regins knew this was showtime. I chose my words carefully, and proposed the invitation in a way Apollo would appreciate it." She winks. "I responded with my future audience:"

Salutations Master Apollo Eirene -

Oh thank, Allah! You are so wise! If I am going to have this event have any influence on these, as you say, privileged prana, I am going to need your help. I know nothing of your advanced and superior ways of living, because I am just a simple Regin yin. How about instead of a ball, we strictly make this a formal gathering. I will have you begin with commencement, and then move into a discussion over dinner; I will have you lead that conversation, and that will be it. No additional frills.

You are an icon at the forefront, highly-merited for your accomplishments, and praised for your triumphant victories during the war-wrenching times our planets will not soon forget. So in honor of not wasting anyone's time, I would be honored to serve with you in this final act of commemorating the end of war with those with true power to make it so.

Will you accept the honor of being my master of ceremony?

Utmost respect,
Lady Cassiopeia Paizo

Apollo nonchalantly said, "Surprised to hear back from Cassiopeia, I got my squad involved. They went wild at belittling this superficial gathering, wishing to cause everyone to feel miserable about their superficial lifestyles. They begged for me to accept, only if they could all get invited too."

Cassiopeia raised an eyebrow. "He would only agree if his entourage came. I reluctantly accepted without—"

Apollo teasingly cuts her off. "Excuse me, Lady Paizo. Don't act so accommodating . . ."

Cassiopeia flashed her coy smile. "Some details might have slipped my mind. I recall wanting more Andromedans to attend. And fortunately his escorts—"

Apollo begins tickling her. "Escorts? You mean my squad who all met two requirements each, young lady!" Cassiopeia taps out. Apollo picks it back up, "My squad qualified, and we accepted our invitations, received our Maresan morph orbs, and were instructed to arrive at Universal Headquarters nine moons early to finalize preparations. Preparations I thought I was prepared for . . ."

Cassiopeia kisses Apollo's cheek as he continues. "I was astonished how quickly word spread, and at the anger toward the requirements to get on the guest list. It caused a scramble that Cassiopeia couldn't frankly have cared less about."

Cassiopeia blurts, "Allah! The Universal Network received complaints about the injustice I'd done unto the elites. They demanded to be invited. On behalf of my intention for the Peace and Unity Ceremony, I was determined to have this event serve a higher purpose than just status. All those within the Universal Network community admired my commitment—except Omega. Determined to attend, he publicly announced that he was going to have his fiancée make an exception."

"Fiancée?" Ariyan and I ask in unison.

Apollo bursts out, "Yeah! It was all over the press!"

Cassiopeia states meekly, "I simply told him he would have to qualify under one of the three requirements. He didn't hold a progressive role, nor was he a leader in education or armed forces. The only requirement he could qualify for was participating in an active relief operation. He scoffed at this, claiming it to be beneath him. Omega bashed, mocked, and made petty comments about everything we'd ever done together. The moment I opened my mouth, he chastised me. Knowing everyone is on their own journey in life, and our only game is to pursue happiness, I wouldn't keep playing next to this loser."

Withholding a smile, Cassiopeia continues, "I ended the conversation tactfully, left the house, and told Ariyan I was moving out. He insisted I stay with him, even joked about how Omega clearly didn't understand how 'no' worked. Finally, he offered me a loft, as close to the Universal Network building as possible. I was just grateful, and still requested that Ariyan come over for dinner. He was a yang to his word. All seemed to remain functional."

Apollo sneaks in, "This caused more gossip to spread. Of course her core team knew the truth, and continued to support Cassiopeia and Ariyan in their actions."

Cassiopeia shrugs. "It was hard for those outside of our core to understand how we carried on, but we knew we could. Regardless of others' understanding, we trusted that the universe was coming together."

Apollo nods. "I think the universe knew it was the perfect era to test our new waters . . . pun intended, my love." He kisses her forehead. Apollo concludes, "Words shape our worlds and our awareness. Our galaxies had moved into peace with open wounds toward misunderstood words. These silent battles had gone unnoticed by warriors like me—those with few words, driven by action."

Cassiopeia emphasized, "That might have been true . . ." She nestles in close to him. "Up until Mares."

Apollo grins. "That's true. That greeting at Universal Network Headquarters on Mares altered history.

9 FIRST IMPRESSIONS

FLASH. I drift above the landing docks at Universal Networks Headquarters, as a hovercraft touches down.

Apollo and his squad had tested out the increase in functionally of their skin suits. Andromedans have a denser central mass, while Maresans are more flexible, with powerful tentacles; this increases their agility, mobility, and stamina. Morph orbs were not needed, just a recommended experience.

The Andromedan squad transformed while making that ride through the galaxy. Since being forced out of active service, had not had any action; this was their first mission back together. Without wanting to act excited, these super mature prana beings started initiating some super important experiments to test out their new suits of arms; complete standard for any serious armed prana being in service. And Apollo's squad was super serious about running only necessary drills to gage their new acquired abilities.

They maturely tested their suction power on every surface, followed by who could crawl the fastest. The experiments discontinued after trying to defy gravity on the ceiling, and attempts to outrun throwing knives—with negative results. Apollo and his squad then bottled back up their curiosities before exiting their hovercraft, never to be seen again—or so they thought.

The Andromedans dock, and join the Regins at the enormous doors of the Main Hall of History. Cassiopeia greets, "Salutations Friends! Welcome to Mares!"

Cassiopeia has met Andromedans before, and thinks they all appreciate whole-hearted embraces; Apollo is not one of these Andromedans. He knows it is a customary greeting to show respect, but he is not planning to show respect at this moment. Once he feels her ultraviolet aura beam hold him, his mind seems to shift instantly. Without meaning to, he generates a cerulean aura that reciprocates her touch, and they instantly swirl in a twisting light.

Apollo has never felt so welcomed in this world. It is the first connection that makes him feel seen. In that moment of acknowledgment, the cerulean frequency vanishes. In his stillness, the dual-colored swirl of affinity is cut short. Apollo shifts backwards, and instantly flickers back into existence.

Cassiopeia teles, *"Did I hurt you?"*

Apollo's squad giggles as Apollo clears his throat and whispers, "In a non-awkward way, I'm never caught off-guard. This—uhh . . . this first impression does not hold true to my character. To be honest, I'm always prepared for all engagements."

"Well in that case," Cassiopeia quietly prys, "you want to give it a second try?"

Disregarding her inquiry, he says, "Enough. Uh, what is your name?"

Cassiopeia smiles, "I am Cassiopeia. We've been in communication."

A bit embarrassed, Apollo fumbles over his words, "Oh! Oh . . . you—you were the one sending me transmissions?" She nods.

Apollo continues, "You were the one who set this up. Huh?" She nods.

"Cool, cool, cool. Okay . . . Take me to your lead for this event? Who is he, anyway?"

A few assistants giggle as Cassiopeia smiles. "That would be me, Cassiopeia. I represent Mares as the director for the Peace and Unity Ceremony; at your service."

Apollo looks shocked, and Cassiopeia teases, "Did that catch you off-guard as well?"

Apollo rubs his neck. "Admittedly, I'm a bit off."

Cassiopeia confidently states, "That's why I'm here. I shall contribute to every part of your creation. You want to have this celebration make an impact, and I believe in all that you speak. I am confident that by me being of service to your vision of this event, we will bring peace and unity to our worlds; trust me. But I must—"

She is interrupted by an anxious messenger. "Cassiopeia, Empress Andromeda needs your guidance. It seems urgent."

Whispers echo from Apollo's squad, *"Drama from the drama queen. What does she want; more advice on how to get a life?"* Before returning to her original thought, Cassiopeia takes notice of Apollo's squad and then of Apollo. He remains at attention, as if he has not heard what was said behind him.

With grace, Cassiopeia continues, "I must attend to customers. Master Apollo, your intention and desired creation will be my top priority. However, if things like this arise, I will see to it that my highly qualified assistant, Julian, is at your service." The most vibrant Maresan steps forward and mouths, *I'm Julian.* Julian shoots Apollo a wink, as Cassiopeia continues, "This event will be an exact reflection of what you truly desire to create. You have my word, for the leve of the universe."

Cassiopeia leaves as teled commotion erupts, *"Rude!" "Did she just reference the universe in vain?" "Leve? What a crude thing to say."* Apollo doesn't entertain their commentary. He heard leve, but thought less about what she said, and more about how she said it. Julian now introduces himself, as well as the assisting staff. Apollo tunes out, but can't help noticing the slight dimming in Cassiopeia's aura as she leaves the group. Julian concludes introductions and proceeds with a tour.

Apollo and his squad explore the first-floor entrance, dining hall, and main hall and hallways. They think they've seen every precious stone and color on the planet Mares, until the Mares Ballroom doors open. They cannot contain their admiration.

The floor of burnt sienna marble finish looks icy slick, but provides firm, warmed suction. All the iridescent panel walls seemed to bow inward, giving guests the feeling of being within a glowing balloon. In the center is a crystal chandelier with scintillating dew drops pooling down from the crystal lights into a natural crystal pool. As everyone marvels at the room, and flabbergasted sounds are released with every turn of the head, Apollo looks around, seeing nothing as impressive as the one who lingers in his mind.

FLASH The story was postponed a bit longer while Apollo clarifies, "Everything extraordinary and incredible to be seen in this building seemed to be overridden by images of Cassiopeia floating in my head. I vaguely remember Julian explaining the Ballroom was where I would give my speech. He pointed up to the open mezzanine, which could be reached by either staircase on the sides. I almost missed the mezzanine part entirely until Julian said I could illuminate or dim the chandelier when drawing in the audience's attention. As Julian continued giving his history lesson of how the most-valued crystals, metals, and minerals were encrusted in that room, my mind had more diplomatic things to resolve; like, '*I wonder what lighting is best for dancing. Does she likes dancing—do I dance? I could dance—I rather like the idea of dancing with her.*'"

FLASH After walking the whole venue, they pick the interior color scheme, followed by the order of entertainment, and move on to choosing the appetizers and dinner options. The process isn't as grueling as Apollo imagined it would be, and by the end, Julian has received a message from Cassiopeia. She has requested to see Apollo—alone.

The message is received very well by Apollo, and he is sure to pull away from his squad. After the dining options are selected, and the agenda structured, Apollo requests his squad disperse to collect intel. They all depart, not to reconvene until dinner.

Once Apollo's squad vacates the Ballroom, Apollo glanced over at Julian, who no longer can muster a straight face. As if he has known Apollo forever, Julian begins to express his excitement—there is true joy in his words. "Oh, my Allah! I have never imagined what a pleasure it would be to create such an impactful moment for our universe! Ha!"

Apollo nonchalantly clarifies, "Look, Julian, I could—"

"Please, call me Jules."

"Okay, Jules. I could care less about creating this frilly ball thing. I don't even know how matching the cakes with the curtains is even important in the long—"

Julian laughs and rolls his eyes. "It's not fair. How is it that you're super attractive and funny?"

Apollo blurts out, "Jules, all Maresans look alike." Facing each other, there were no obvious features that stood out. Other than the sleeveless green fitted dress that Apollo was wearing, complimentary to the shoulder-padded red dress on Julian, they looked identical—even their skin tone.

Jules joviality agrees, "Absolutely! And we all look fabulous! Simplicity at its finest; evolution isn't necessary beyond this form." He twirls like a mop with an oversized handle nub and eyes. Truthfully this description did not do Julian justice. After the third pirouette-like spin he rose to the tops of his tentacles elevating himself almost a meter off the ground. Then all at once, he stopped abruptly with the help of his powerful suction cups he stuck his landing effortlessly.

Julian continued, "I know how you must think me a very simple being, and I agree. The truth is Maresans are simple, because we in habitat the easiest planet to live on in any galaxy. We have the most accepting atmosphere—and the most radiant sky! Beyond costume aesthetics, the only thing that alters is that the cranial processor enlarges. Your morph orbs are not needed, just highly recommended to experience an enlarged brain. I hear the Universal Network wants to enhance the Maresan experience to other planets. Ariyan was saying that the UN is thinking about colonizing a group on planet Arth for testing."

Apollo panics, "Are there any side effects— with this brain?"

Julian thinks, and then responds, "Well, you might overthink concepts of little control—common ones I've heard from previous guests were along the lines of perfection . . . and the meaning of life. That's about it. You just question a lot more things that you just use to accept."

Apollo hesitates. "You mean all these questions and distracting thoughts I have now are normal for you? I feel . . . conflicted. Are you sure I'm not doing it wrong?"

Jules eases his immediate concern. "Shhhhh . . . There is no wrong. And free-flowing thought is normal, and slightly distracting. Look, you just focus on what you are feeling; Cassiopeia will do the rest. You *don't think you* know what you want, but you do have an idea. And whatever you *think* it should look like, she already sees it."

Julian is nodding, while Apollo stays stationary. "Don't worry—I'm with you," Jules reassures. "I have no idea how she does it all, but the moment you walk into this Ballroom on the evening of the Celebration, you're gonna be like, 'How did she get inside of my head?' I see it happen, every time with everyone she works with." Julian keeps nodding, while Apollo now appears unsettled.

Julian exclaims, "Allah, for someone who is about to impact the universe, you are one of very few words." He looks around as if he does not want anyone to hear, and then leans back in toward Apollo. "And to think, we will be impacting the elites of the entire universe." Julian doesn't see Apollo cringe at his sincerity. Apollo's grimacing attitude is short-lived as Julian states, "Okay! It's showtime; off to Cassiopeia."

They both step through the doorway, down a narrow hallway leading to a courtyard. Right before they reach the soil, Julian turns towards staircase leading to the rooftop of this three-story building. Julian begins to ascend, and about midway, Apollo sees a miniature oasis beside a small resting bench.

Sitting on the bench is a peaceful Cassiopeia. She breaks her gaze out over the courtyard, to acknowledge Julian with a smile. She then lends her attention to Apollo, who now ascends much quicker, as if he's racing; Apollo takes the prize. Cassiopeia gestures toward Julian that he may depart.

Julian exits. "I shall see you both at dinner."

Cassiopeia returns to Apollo's unwavering gleam a moment longer. Silence is broken once Cassiopeia stands and begins with, "Hello."

Apollo sarcastically says, "*Just* hello. No offense, but you didn't have to get me alone just to greet me."

Cassiopeia squints a bit. "Well, I wasn't sure. I don't want to make it a habit of you getting nervous around me." Apollo burst out in uncontrollable laughter, causing Cassiopeia to join in. They regain control, and Cassiopeia gestures to continue up the stairs. As he ascends, he thinks about what he said to Julian. It was true—Maresans all look alike, but there's no denying that she was uniquely Cassiopeia.

Once they successfully reach the top of the stairs, side by side, they head to the ledge of the rooftop. Apollo starts it up, "So, were you able to keep Empress Andromeda cooled enough not to lose her feathers? I imagine working with a phoenix wouldn't be easy."

Cassiopeia responds, "I don't talk about my customers, unless it is necessary. What I want to know is what is taking place in your universe." Leaning toward a low-hanging sun, both feel it's much closer to setting than either of them wants.

191

"So," Cassiopeia leads in, "what's it feel like to be considered god-like in these galaxies?"

"No one's ever asked me such a question before," Apollo admits. Cassiopeia was somewhat teasing, but truly was inspired by his life. She didn't dare speak this truth, in fear of jeopardizing the upcoming ceremony; so she played it cool. With her loyalty to the cause, she was committed to not having her emotions taint divinity.

Apollo does not know how to respond, until he looks into Cassiopeia's eyes. In just a few seconds, he realizes he has a longing to be heard. He takes a deep breath and responds, in pure and unrecognized vulnerability, "Lonely."

The moment Apollo utters the word, a surprising fear rushes over him. It's present, but not paralyzing. He remains in complete safety of Cassiopeia's eyes. Cassiopeia purses her lips. "Thank you for your honesty. I must confess, I too am lonely." She appears relieved to express her thoughts, sharing fully, "The first time I was asked if I needed anything, I realized I didn't, but being surrounded by two dozen in need. That's when I first heard someone screaming for purpose—without uttering one word. When I discovered I was the only one who heard it, I realized my purpose was to guide others to seek what they needed—but not a typical guide—I am a guide for inner voices."

Apollo shook his head, "Inner voices? I don't understand."

Cassiopeia smiles, "I can hear the true desires hidden within all those around me; even you. I hear the truest calls longing to realign within their misaligned universes." Cassiopeia looks at him with tender eyes and reveals, "I listen for the hearts who share their desires that are no longer being pursued by the vessels they are within. See, I serve as a liaison by first reflecting the desire, then echoing it, and finally—"

Apollo rushes in, "What does mine look—errr . . . sound like? Do we share similar desires? I mean, are we compatible—errr . . . do you like to dance?"

Cassiopeia shies away. "Well, I . . . well. I don't really know what mine says." She almost looks embarrassed. "I do this for everyone, but can't seem to do it for me."

Apollo persists, "Seriously?" He forgets about himself—for once—and focused on her, "You don't know what your own heart desires . . . Why is that?"

Cassiopeia bites her bottom lip, "There are hearts with much louder desires to be heard than mine. Yours included."

Apollo is taken aback. As he thinks about what that must be like, he returns to wondering about his deepest desire. Before he thinks too long, Cassiopeia takes a deep breath and begins to radiate a violet glow. He scuttles back a bit.

Vulnerably, Cassiopeia explains, "I provide a voice for every heart who come see me; most don't even know I'm doing it, even though I'm doing it all the time."

Subtly, a little seed of light forms and floats between her lifted appendages. The glowing seedling starts to pulse like a heartbeat: Bum-bum.

Bum-bum. She elaborates, "This seedling represent's an unheard heart's echo. My heart hears what it needs in order to be seen by my customer. My aura then seeks my customer's aura and finds at least two, most of the time three, desired outcomes that would have my customer realign with their heart's desire and be left satisfied with my services.

Apollo observes that the seedling appears to be one with Cassiopeia as she continues, "I begin by influencing an environment around what my customers desires to seek out of life, based on what they need—not just want. This environment is kept separate initially; I do not introduce my customer until they are ready. Otherwise it will be too much of a distraction—overwhelming, if you will." Other seedlings appear and begin drifting around both her and Apollo. They all look similar, but they only engage with one another. None approach the single initial seedling. A few are violet; most others are aqua blue or kelly green.

Cassiopeia continues, "My customers all seem to know how they are seen; rarely do they know who they wish to be seen as. That is where I come in. I have a gift to know how they wish to be seen. When working with them, I have their actions always speak louder than their words." Slowly her aura color alters to an aqua blue, and all the other seeds remain the same—except for the first little seed of light floating between her tentacles. It matches her blue glow.

"Too often, prana say one thing but mean another… in fear of admitting what they really want is also a hidden need. They believe they can hide it, but that is where your heart has been calling from; that is where I will go." Now her aura color drops down to a kelly green, and so does the seed of light. Apollo is puzzled, but not more than he is curious.

Cassiopeia continues, "No matter how long it takes, eventually a choice will be made. All choices are available, and one will lead them to follow their true desire." Cassiopeia remains kelly green, as the seedlings morphs multiple times, as if making an ultimate choice. It goes to violet and blue, then back to green—then remain violet. Cassiopeia seems collected, and sighs with the final color. The little lights that surround her tentacles gravitate toward the little seed in the center and begin to pulsate.

"Once a customer sees that they want the want just as equally as they want the need, I know it's time for them to enjoy their own environment with fresh eyes—and their performance truly begins." The violet seedling drifts out of the protection of her tentacles, and into the middle of the other lights. "Only then do they give *themselves* a chance to observe the different life choices they have been given. And without feeling obligated, they play around with the different directions to find their heart's truest desire. More often than not, my customers embrace the gift their heart was seeking, and align it with their new lifestyle. Moving forward, they continue cultivating their environment in the direction of their newfound alignment."

All of a sudden, the aqua blue and kelly green lights fade away, and Cassiopeia's green aura does as well. All the violet lights orbit the seedling for a bit, before it joins in the circling orbit. They form a solid-looking halo, which slowly enlarges to create a large ring around both Cassiopeia and Apollo. Both their eyes lock, before the violet circle suddenly dims out.

Apollo questions, "Why do they choose one?"

Cassiopeia giggles a bit at his question, until she realizes he is serious. "Well, we always choose something—even if it's indecision. Prana beings living life always have a path. Left or right, both are walkways. To not choose a direction would be like standing at the crossroad, staring at a wall."

Cassiopeia investigates, "Were you taught about your labyrinth?" Apollo shakes his head no. She exclaims, "Wow. Our galaxies are different. Let me try to explain the game of life." She places her tentacles on Apollo's shoulders. "I was taught that prana need to let go and flow. Life is just a game, a labyrinth if you will. Choices create movement through our elaborate pathways and dead ends. Each move gets us closer, or eliminates uncertainty of where we want to go; indecision does not. Prana brings choosing stagnation in flow, hoping for stability and security, only build up disconnection among the universal cosmos. I know; I did it for eighteen levels. Resisting the unknown only grows fear. Fear is resistance, and what we resist will persist. It's peculiar that not until fear is let go, do w—"

Apollo finishes the thought, "Do we understand that we do not lose ourselves."

"Accurate," Cassiopeia confirms.

Apollo shakes his head. "In the Andromeda galaxy, I was taught something similar: Become your own flow, always let go. I was taught there is no use in

196

holding on, but I have to admit I'm still afraid of losing things. I'm not gonna lie, I don't trust that divinity will keep the right things around. My old captain once told me, 'By Allah, you aren't capable of losing anything, because—'"

Cassiopeia recites toward the sun, "You cannot lose what is truly yours. Yeah, same here; I haven't fully trusted divinity since . . . I first left Chivalry."

Apollo gains clarity. "Our previous teachings reflect from similar areas. To be honest, I don't fully understand this labyrinth, but I do understand that it's no fun to stare at a wall. Especially when there are other things to be mesmerized by . . ."

Cassiopeia begins laughing at the thought that he might be flirting with her. He laves hearing her laugh. She recites, "I mark you free from ever being deterred by another, by bestowing unto you an expression of unconditional bliss: To leve is to live. To live is to flow. To flow is to give. To give is to grow. In all of our moments, this we must know."

Apollo tries to relate, "I know it must be hard to live in a world of leve. I was born with a heart of lava, and yearn to feel the heat of the moment, if you know what I mean. It just seems so restricting; one partner—if that! And you all seem so prude. It seems hard to imagine this being a life anyone would choose. No offense."

She turns to lean back over the ledge. Perplexed by his sharing, Cassiopeia clarifies, "Yes, well . . . I will retract any distasteful feelings toward your lava-filled words. To be honest, my customers from your galaxy are much more risqué than I ever thought imaginable, but they do cause me to question my opinions . . . sometimes. It quiet perplexing to engage in showing lava to someone you care deeply for; and the idea of showing intense emotions to multiple partners is overwhelming! Until being forced to leave Chivalry, I had only heard of lava, but never experienced it. I explained my feelings of lava to your Empress Andromeda once, and she told me I needed to embrace it."

Dismissing Cassiopeia's clearly mixed emotions in misunderstanding lava, Apollo rolls his eyes and begins on a minor tangent "I cannot believe you have to work with her. In a non-awkward way, I lava that I get to work with you, but I leve that I am helping plan this party on her behalf . . . I've never even talked to her—for good reason, I'll have you know. I don't know why she sucked me into this." Feeling only self-pity for himself, Apollo now looks over at Cassiopeia, realizes she was still talking. "Oh! I apologize. Were you done?"

Cassiopeia chuckles, "No, no. That's quite alright. I'm quite happy with the way this is working out. I am glad she chose you to work with me on this. Of course, I understand you might have reservations from previous experiences, but we will work through them. And perhaps it's time for me to embrace this feeling of lava, because I still feel it. Sometimes." She looks outward. "I feel it sometimes, this lava. When I walk around these buildings, I feel it toward myself. I become disconnected. I invest endless amounts of effort making connections, trying to find where I flow in the universe. But the moment I am by myself, it dissipates, drying up."

Apollo remembers Cassiopeia's aura dimming down as she left the hovercraft docks. He doesn't bring it up. Instead he shares, "To be honest, I feel like you're speaking to parts of me that I've always felt, but never shared." With the purest of intentions, he rests his top two right tentacles on hers, which are resting on the ledge. He declares, "I am here. You are not alone." They look at one another and both feel it—the moment their loneliness is no longer present.

Cassiopeia begins again, "Sir Apollo. This seems very out of your character."

Apollo responds, "Perhaps you just bring out the sides of me I never share."

Cassiopeia sees a twinkle in his eyes. She asks, "So, what's it feel like to know I consider you god-like in my universe?"

This time, Apollo looks into Cassiopeia's eyes, and finds a smoldering fire that ignites his soul. Now, with embers, he responds with, "I feel powerful." They hold this moment present as the sun touches the horizon. Both are aware and turn their attention on it as it sets. They hold on to eternity together. The sun disappears. Cassiopeia's still face melts to reveal her coy smile.

Apollo recites the famous Sir Reginald, "In all my moments, I choose to stay in this one forever."

Cassiopeia laughs as she delivers lines of Lady Andromeda, "I do not wish to be the restraint or downfall on this determined star that is destined to become a legend by all those who follow . . ."

At that moment, Apollo grabs her tentacles, making it clear that he intends to kiss her. As he initiates by drawing nearer to her, Cassiopeia, who is swept up in the moment, tries to give in.

Cassiopeia no knowing how to melt into another gracefully is a bit rigid, and uncertain of the customs of intimacy; physical contact is a very taboo within her current understanding of leve, Cassiopeia entrusts Apollo with her whole being, and he reciprocates a mutual intention. Feeling sincerely vulnerable, Apollo whispers unapologetically, "I think I lava you." This causes Cassiopeia to recoil, and slip out of his grasp.

Sounding hurt Cassiopeia asks, "How could one say that?"

Apollo shrugs, "It's easy. I've nothing to lose."

Cassiopeia retorts, "The feeling is not mutual. Perhaps your brute stature only knows malice and war! Lava festers, erupts, and violently destroys. Where's the leve?"

Apollo steps back, "Oh, I would never dream of saying leve to a creature such as yourself! I am a warrior of honor! There's legacy in my lava line. Leve is a placid word for those lacking true feeling. Leve drowns out lava and keeps the masses separate. No offense, but everyone knows that."

Cassiopeia scolds, "I should expect an ignorant description to come from a barbaric animmel living within a testosterone-driven land. No respect for consent, just a bag of cheap words and lack of respect for others."

Very confused if he'd insulted her, Apollo tries again, "I know it might be hard for you to comprehend, but what I am saying is I don't fault you for your use of primitive language. Let me show you what your life could be like if enhanced." He moves in and tries to embrace her.

Cassiopeia wriggles back. "I have not given consent, and decline your advances and inappropriate enhancements!"

Apollo pleads, "But we are called to each other. I can feel it—my lava erupts for you, and I know yours does as well. It's obvious that you are just denying yourself of embracing it! Come on, Cassio—"

Cassiopeia clarifies, "Your emotions are not to be trusted, especially when wanting to take actions that force yourself into another's world." Cassiopeia purses her lips and then declares, "I am here to serve, to fulfill the services needed by assistants and guests. Fulfilling wants is not on my agenda. It might serve you well if you choose to do the same." She almost looks unsure of what she has said.

Seeming dazed, Apollo states, "Come, now. Surely we both want this. I can sense that we—"

Cassiopeia looks him flat in the face with much clarity, "I will not engage in this behavior with you." She returns her gaze to the horizon and speaks informatively, "I do not mean to offend you, but I think there is more to our paths crossing. Respectfully, please allow me to fulfill this celebration." Apollo almost refutes, but chooses not to.

So much of what Apollo wants is for her to reconsider, but his pride spews out. "I have said all I need to. I shall rejoin my squad for dinner. I have spent much time without accomplishing anything, and I will no longer waste it here. I will call upon you when your assistance is needed." Apollo descends without giving her a chance to say anything.

Not wanting to seem hurt, he refrains from conversations and eye contact while in the dining room. Dinner is presented; Cassiopeia isn't present. As dinner unfolds, Apollo's squad pieces together Cassiopeia's engagement to Ariyan's oldest yin. Gossip flies like mad throughout the meal. Trying not to care isn't working, so he tries to lessen her allure by intensifying his disgust for her. Apollo formulates that Cassiopeia was after personal gain, and that she only assisted in the creation of this event for her own claim to fame. These thoughts mill around in his head, until she enters the room. All malicious thoughts are dashed away as Apollo's aura once again begins to swoon. Over two dozen beings are present, but it feels like just the two of them.

As Cassiopeia finds her seat, she apologizes, "I'm sorry for my tardiness. Ariyan has informed me he will not be in attendance during the planning and preparation phase. Fortunately, he will return for the celebration. Now that we've all seen the venue and picked all the . . ."

As she continues to speak, Apollo is in wonder at how she doesn't even seem phased; not even a little disrupted. Could he be so far off as to how she felt toward him? He tunes back in. "So every evening will end just like this one: Dinner followed by the next day's agenda. You will find that—"

It hits Apollo that he has a few days to prove to her that he is the one. He just needs an opening to prove it to her. Cassiopeia finishes up, "Finally, sleeping arrangements. You all will be accommodated in the commune adjacent from Headquarters. Everyone who arrived yesterday, feel free to do as you'd like. Andromedans, we will head there after dinner, once you grab your belongings."

In the morning, Cassiopeia greets Apollo with four solid knocks on his door. Cheerfully, she begins, "Morning, morning! Are you ready for an incredible day?"

Apollo goes from a smoldering look to acting confused, "Do I have a choice?"

She jokingly adds, "You always have a choice, silly. Now, would you rather start with the hard stuff, or—"

Apollo gets really close to her. "Well, it depends on what you consider hard." Cassiopeia holds her position, but inches backward. She calmly answers, "Well, choosing the plasma containers might be most difficult in your case." Apollo is caught off-guard, as she continues inching backward. "We have to pick a chalice so memorable that they take it with them from the Grand Ballroom into the Dining Room . . . It has to be practical, with elegance that elevates the ambiance, but not distracting."

Apollo has never thought about a cup so much, nor does he want to. "Yeah. No offense, but that's not my idea of hard stuff. What I thought would be fun to do . . ." He grabs one of Cassiopeia's tentacles, and she slaps him hard with three others.

203

He retracts, "What is your deal? To be honest, I just wanted to—"

"Perhaps the hard stuff for you will be understanding self-control," Cassiopeia spits out.

Apollo is flabbergasted. "Really? Allah, you Regins are so stuck up. It was a compliment."

Cassiopeia retorts, "Wow, and you Andromedans sure think highly of yourself. Do you really think yourself so honorable that you are called to our primitive galaxy to show us your righteous ways?"

Apollo doesn't want to agree. "Well . . . to be honest, I wouldn't say called . . . as much as transmitted; but Regins do seem to have things backwards here. It's like y'all cringe at the idea of connection. In a non-awkward way, I was just trying to help you."

Cassiopeia laughs and then stares blankly. "Wow. Just wow. Connection is not just physical. But I don't know . . . maybe that's how lava is programmed, aye?"

Apollo shrugs. "I mean, it doesn't have to be, but it makes it more fun."

Cassiopeia nods. "Well, what would you say to someone like me who thought the most fun to have with an equal counterpart is long conversations about Self-discoveries and personal growth?"

Apollo tries not to laugh. "To be honest, I'd say let's pump some lava into that!"

Cassiopeia purses her lips. "Let's get started with today's schedule, shall we?" She pulls out a list.

"We must complete this list by this evening. By lunch, we can—"

Apollo cuts her off, "Wait, we're not done with this conversation. Don't tell me I hurt your feelings again. No offense, but you're way too sensitive."

Cassiopeia does not answer his questions. "I say we should start with the easy stuff; table decorations. By lunch, we will be meeting with the entertainment and preparing their tech equipment. Got it?"

Apollo sounds hurt. "That's it? Are you not going to answer me?"

With a poised face, Cassiopeia restates, "I will keep our conversations short, and my Self-growth stunted to accommodate you. I only ask that you please refrain from making contact with me, Master Eirene. Do you understand?"

Feeling wounded by his pride being put in its place, Apollo confirms, "Got it."

That day, and for all that follow, Cassiopeia appears to play the role of his personal shadow. Whatever he needs, he needs no longer. Cassiopeia is best at serving, and she continues to function at a flawless level of mastery, despite the whispers of Apollo's squad: "*She must be up to something.*" "*I wonder when she's going to break? She is only doing this to take over after Ariyan passes on to the next dimension.*" "*If she'd care this much for her poor betrothed Iava, she could've saved her relationship.*" "*How does Apollo put up with her two-facedness?*"

Apollo despises how easily she denies all his acts of endearment. She's made this whole process so difficult for him, especially in the moments they are together. He is drawn to her.

Every morning after, Cassiopeia greets him with a smile. He now will only cast a dismissive nod, or bark a belittling comment. She does not react; she just indicates she heard him. She will try to walk beside him, but he will thrust himself slightly ahead of her. That is their routine; it is not ideal, but it suits him.

Throughout the day, Apollo will attempt to become affectionate, and she rejects all his attempts to become close. Eventually, he creates distance; it is not ideal, but it suits her.

Cassiopeia has committed herself to him as if she is his shadow. She fulfills all his desires, from the morning greeting to the evening adieu. She satisfies all appropriate requests without hesitation; it is not ideal, but it is the only way she knows how to leve. Cassiopeia keeps her distance from her own longing desire; she too is drawn to him. Unknowingly to both, Cassiopeia is inspiring Apollo's commencement speech. It really isn't a surprise to anyone who knows Apollo, except for him, but he has not been on his slander wagon since he arrived. Unadmitted by Apollo, he's had other things on his mind . . . Well, one thing. Her. Cassiopeia has always been on his mind.

The evening before the celebration, all arrangements are finalized. Apollo is feeling content about himself and what's to come next. He begins fantasizing about completing his speech and everyone clamoring over him, telling him how much they adore him and how he inspired them to change their ways. Then he remembers who will be in attendance; then he cringes about swimming with all those self-entitled entities. He clear his thoughts, and focuses on who he'll want to swim with. Cassiopeia pops up; only her.

It's this thought that has him want to leave immediately. Why? Well, he thinks leaving immediately afterward will be easier than asking the questions he's afraid to answer. Apollo is caught in such turmoil: *If leve is such a revolting thing, then why do I feel lava?* Much like a muse to an artist, Cassiopeia lingers on his thoughts, and has him reaching for understanding, especially when his thoughts return to his speech. The speech he wrote to blatantly ridicule the audience, belittle Mares, and feel justified in his wants to start the war back up. But the truth is. . . Apollo no longer felt aligned with his speech.

The way Apollo felt about the occurrences that had led up to today, since he arrived on Mares had him question what he really wanted to get out of his current words he planned on spreading. His words were filled with so much superiority in his ways . . . well, his old ways of thinking. If it wasn't for this ceremony and speech, he would have never met or lived any other outside of Andromedan culture. Perhaps that would have suited him, but knowing of Cassiopeia, or felt convicted to understand someone he felt so misunderstood by. These thoughts had him questioning his ideals of truth, ultimately altering his universe, and giving in to the ideas that maybe there was different ways to lava and live life. Maybe things are not as complicated; could life be simple?

Apollo quickly snapped out of it, and returned to his state of being absolutely correct . . . for now. And like most great influencers, he got right back to procrastinating on changing anything in his one-tracked narrative within his speech.

10 THE CELEBRATION

The morning of the celebration starts off very differently for Apollo. It's not Cassiopeia who greets him. The door bursts open, "Salutations Apollo! Gewd Morgan; I hope you're ready for—"

Apollo jumps back. "Woah, woah! Ever heard of knocking. And Jules . . . since when do you say 'gewd morgan'?"

Julian pauses. "Well, I did my own research and saw popular ways for Andromedans to be greeted in the morning! I went with the no-frills pronunciation." Julian's nodding, while Apollo stays stationary.

Jules picks it back up, "Well, I guess I should have asked what you prefer . . . Anyway, anyway! I'm taking the lead today. Cassiopeia will be behind the scenes. Ariyan will introduce you—he does apologize for his absence for the majority of your visit . . ."

As Julian continues on, Apollo now realizes that by avoiding Cassiopeia tonight, he might never see her again. His fear of loss is rocked. Is he being too hasty in leaving immediately? If he leaves without trying, will he miss his shot? Well, if this is his shot, he should take it. But where? Where does he want to take it? Behind the scenes! But will she still be there? Well, the one way to find out is to go. Staying in this conversation with Julian is not going to help him find her. Apollo tunes back in as Julian concludes, "So besides the run-through rehearsal before lunch—"

Apollo cuts him short, "That all sounds delightful. Besides eating, is there anything else I must attend to today?"

Julian thinks. "No, just what you'll wear for—"

Apollo concludes, "Splendid. It's already handled! See you at breakfast! Tah, tah!"

"Oh! Apollo, one more thing! How would you like to be announced tonight?"

Apollo sarcastically states, "Lady Cassiopeia said it best, 'The most honorable being called to this galaxy; Sir Apollo Eirene.'"

Apollo slams the door, exiting out of his washroom window and out of the commune. He runs about half a kilometer before questioning why he's running. No one's chasing him, and by the next moon, he will be long gone. It is here that he gains clarity. For the first time, thinking about what could happen, he imagines paths. Knowing he had a whole life before Cassiopeia that he could keep living, but rather than returning to that, he would rather keep fighting her in the name of lava, against her leve, because he accepts that she's insane for not seeing his point. He's uncertain what path he will take, but he's certain that he wants to thank all those who have assisted him during his stay.

Not wanting to be misunderstood, he begins giving gratitude toward all those who helped manifest this most sonder event; he even starts hearing lava in their leve. The conversations aren't long, but are all telling:

Apollo will say, "Thank you so much for helping me. I typically leve these things . . ."

The assistant will say, "We leve to serve, honestly."

Apollo will ask, "Is there anything else that you have planned in life?"

The assistant will say, "Go do something else that makes me happy."

Apollo asks, "What makes you happy?"

The assistant will often say, "Being of service when I'm off the o'clock. I leve working, but I enjoy this free time. I never know what I will discover about myself with each event, ceremony, or celebration I attend."

After the twentieth time Apollo gets told this, he starts to appreciate the consistency and how genuine Maresans are about Self-discovery. He discovers that all who are working the event are doing so outside of their careers.

Most of these assistants work at schools, as consultants, or as brand ambassadors. He finds that those assisting as kitchen sages, custodial artists, live performers, and floor hosts all have very complex and fascinating lives outside of the hours he witnesses them dedicating for tonight's celebration.

By the end of his afternoon, Apollo almost starts saying leve. Feeling comfortable about being with others, he wonders if he'd be comfortable being by her without forcing himself on her. His mind shifts again: *Where is she? How could I have missed her?*

Throughout the day, Apollo was sure he'd see her. He was ashamed to say he had no reason to beckon on her. His only excuse would have been that he needed her, but all the tasks she had were done, or reassigned already. Whispers of her still traveled around: *"She never comes to these events." "Always preparing, never partying." "She must be too ashamed of herself to ever show her face" "What does Ariyan think of her?"*

The event finally comes to fruition. To soothe his nerves, Apollo runs through his welcoming salutations again and again. Once he is sure he's primed up, he enters the ballroom as if walking onto a battlefield he will conquer. Nothing could prepare him for what he walks in on. As he enters the decadently prim and polished venue, he is humbled. It's everything he imagined, without even knowing it. He looks at all the tapestries, and not one silk thread is out of place. He hears elegant melodies, smells rich aromas, and the instant he stops looking for something to ridicule for being even slightly out of place, he sees the reflection of himself in the crystal fountain. He wishes to disappear. As Apollo walks through the crowd, it's as if all the conversations he has echoing inside of his head are amplified on all the guests' lips.

The guests are rambling all his not-so-secret thoughts: *"Can you believe they let him in here? Wasn't he discharged for being too full of himself?"* *"Could I get promoted if I take command of one of* the traveling paramedics' troops? If not, what is the point?" "I hear the Regins are still way behind on the latest trends; pathetic." "Do you think I could become a commanding officer with you even if I never was sent into battle?" Boisterous remarks echo and boom off the ballroom and hallway walls, resting on his ear holes.

As he strolls by his squad, they don't even notice him. They've found other colleagues who gladly gawk at and ridicule the event. He overhears many prana buzzing about collaborating, strictly to better themselves. He has never heard such dramatically different conversations happening in one place, except in his mind. The same types of conversations overlapping; multiple times in different tones.

Several guests, ranging from advisors to admirals, now approach him—not to gossip, or in hopes of collaborating after the conclusion of the ceremony. No, these guests are curious about the service he was gifted by Cassiopeia. They wish to genuinely congratulate him on his enchanting venue. They ask one of three things: "Was this everything you imagined; what it was like working with her?", "Did she detail it to the exact image you had in your mind?", "Do you know if she already has another customer?"

FLASH. Apollo breaks out of character again, "I must have seemed out of place to guests, but I had no idea what they were going on about; and I didn't want to seem ignorant by asking what she had done for them, so I continued to feel foolish in all of these

213

conversations. I was not prepared for these types of questions, and at this point of the evening, I had no idea what was to come from this event."

"You could have asked," Cassiopeia points out.

Apollo nods. "In hindsight, yes, but I stand by my defensive approach of not letting them know I had no idea of what was going on. I used my evasive tactics to navigate their conversations."

Cassiopeia giggles, "For someone who was so willing to slander all these guests behind their backs, I'm surprised you didn't want a certain reputation to be had."

Apollo puts his hand across his heart. "By Allah, during those conversations, I still felt righteous within my opinions. I am glad I spoke with Empress Andromeda. It was only then that the righteous feelings faltered."

FLASH. Apollo sees a light beam brightly toward him. Soon, her aura dims and he can see a voluptuous yin saunter forward. She is bold and demands the attention in the room. She chose to wear an Arth capsule for the evening, adorned in a fitted, sleeveless, gaudy sequin-covered jumpsuit with a translucent shawl cascading over. It looks to be made of the finest metallic silks. As she enters the hall, Apollo can now tell this is the Empress; lava or leve her, she is untouchable. And apparently, the Empress intends on introducing herself to Apollo.

"Salutations, Apollo." Empress Andromeda chooses a most soothing telepathic tone, removing the need to raise her tone in the noisy ballroom. *"You*

must feel like the luckiest bachelor in the entire galaxy. To have the lady of the universe here at your service, but only for this short time. Please tell me, and I do hope you will—what were Cassiopeia's parting words with you? And do go into detail!"

Andromeda looks around, and then leans in to whisper softly in his ear with a tone that has a bite, "She has such a way with parting words and sharp messages." She takes a step back, grants him a wink as if she really wants that part to stand out, and begins to tele again, *"I really hope you didn't make the mistake of trying to coerce her to be with you— you dreamboat, you. I've heard about your scandalous reputation. Oh, but Allah, I don't mind! Allah knows, I think it's more fun to dive in when the lava is hot. Your wild flames were probably too much for her . . . I don't think Cassiopeia understands lava."*

Not quite sure how Andromeda knows any of this, Apollo allows Andromeda to unravel. *"She was spouting off about leve, like she doesn't know how absurd that word is. I don't know how long you put up with it. I did my best—but even I need to get away from such negativity once in a while. These prudes with their monogamy. They would do well to mix things up, like us. Everyone needs to embody the melting pot. The Regins tried, but toward the end, even Cassiopeia was asking me to explain what it would mean for an Andromedan to confess lava toward a Regin."* She glances around and then back to Apollo. *"I heard things might have gotten off to a rocky start the first evening with you two. I'm suspicious if she's fallen in lava with one of your squad mem—"*

Apollo cuts her off. "Empress Andromeda, please excuse me, but I am afraid that is a horrendous rumor. Cassiopeia's name should never be spoken with such slander. Now, unless you have some imperative information, then I suggest you go and enjoy your environment and your party guests."

Empress Andromeda scoffs, "My guests? My environment? Apollo? Reality check, please! Are you speaking at this celebration, or am I? This is not my environment. Do you think I would have picked this chalice and curtain combination? Nay-nay-nay. You did; this is your play box, my dearest lava. I am only here as your guest of honor and you ought to—"

Apollo almost corrects her that it was the cakes with the curtains, but then shakes his head, realizing that she's right. He tries to gain traction. "But you chose me. This isn't mine. I didn't . . . I'm not her . . ."

The Empress seems to pity him. "Oh, my! You have been swooning far too much here. You better snap to it. The event has started, the performance has begun, and *you* are suited as the keynote speaker. You cannot let Cassiopeia down. She casted you for this performance. I'm counting on you, and so is she. She has a reputation for delivering top-notch shows."

The Empress scans Apollo and begins a slow, continuous nod. "What? Did she not prompt you with enough clues, my little seedling?" Apollo considers that maybe this was for him. He looks around and finally admits that Jules was right . . . She did get inside of his head, but Julian said nothing about getting inside his heart. He takes it all in, before looking back at the Empress. She giggles and teles, *"My, you are magnificent at seeming to . . . just wing it."* Apollo becomes enlightened about what this must mean—Cassiopeia trusts him to follow his heart and choose a direction. He is no longer going to be indecisive.

Apollo pieces it together. He's her current customer. His desire was to disrupt life, and he's now aware that he had a choice of how he wants to see others, and be seen by others going forward.

Now he understands why he was to be the keynote speaker for this performance. Laughter fills his soul and bursts out of him when it becomes clear that those who approached him earlier knew what it meant for him to have been working with her—what this event really represented for him. He looks around the room, enamored by what he sees. This is his environment. All the conversations are the conversation currently happening in his head. Here stands Apollo, this elite galactic leader—who speaks with such authority, wanting this epic change of the self-entitled prana. Apollo, the leader in his own hypocrisy, who thinks so highly of himself, while looking down on his own reflection. Could he still become that god-like leader he so badly wants to be? Apollo knows he's center stage; not the center of attention, but the center of intention.

Apollo becomes present to the seeds of light Cassiopeia showed him. He thinks about the guests and the necessary requirements. These guests are not their titles, but rather their looped conversations they represent. His party is full of his favorite three topics: ridicule for recognition, seeking allevelated growth for gratification, and wanting to make a difference. With a new frame of mind, Apollo begins to view this event as a performance piece perfectly crafted by the mastermind known as Cassiopeia. He looks around and for the first time recognizes that everyone who is assisting is playing Cassiopeia; each guest is none other than he.

All guests are reflections of Apollo—the elite galactic leaders, who came to planet Mares to bring greatness with no humility. He pans his focus to where his self-entitled greatness first began on this planet—the greeting.

Each guest is met with a whirl of light and affinity, automatically followed by shrills of laughter and delight through a heartfelt connection right off the bat. All the hosting greeters beam with the same enchantment that Cassiopeia first casted on him. A rush of understanding falls over Apollo, and he gets it. She pierced through him, quicker than anyone. She demonstrated to those assisting how to greet prana who genuinely want to connect without knowing it. Observing from afar, he hasn't realized how much he needed that.

Apollo underestimated Cassiopeia's wit. Having him be the demonstration granted everyone alike the ability to find connection. Every prana in attendance now knows the experience of being seen; even those who did not know they needed it.

Apollo sighs and teles Empress Andromeda, as he nods toward the main entrance, *"I can wing it, because she knows she gave me wings. She trusts me."* They both watch as one guest blips out of existence, and then reappears moments later, filled with delight.

Andromeda clarifies, *"Ah! That's what I call, 'lava at first sight.' It doesn't happen too much anymore."*

Apollo directs his attention back to the Empress, but she does not break her gaze from the delighted guest. "What ever do you mean?"

Andromeda elaborates telepathically, *"Greetings in the Reginald galaxy are often too rigid. It ruffles my feathers. This pretend illusion of wanting to connect, while remaining guarded. Only when both parties are willing to connect will that flowing light sync up to the same aura frequency."*

Apollo shakes his head. "I'm afraid you missed that—that prana disappeared."

Andromeda laughs, squawking. "If that prana disappeared, then how are they there?" She points directly at the being sashaying across the floor. "Did you think they *literally* disappeared? Why you—oh, darling! I'm glad you're willing to be ignorant now, and not remain a fool! Hmm . . . I guess rigid greetings still happen in our galaxy." She laughs even harder.

Apollo seems a bit crushed, but still enlightened in his curiosity, "Well . . . yes. I thought *I* had disappeared, but I didn't. I get that now; so where did I go?"

Andromeda indicates for him to lean forward, then she sneaks a kiss on his check. "You did go . . . you let go, and created duality." She leans back out. "You simply became the opposite—it's very common to lose oneself the first time you are willing to allow someone to see you. You remove everything in the way, and create transparency with another being. What you witnessed wasn't prana disappearing. It might have appeared that way to you, but there were still two aura lights in tango. The brighter one took the lead, while the other followed suit. Like magic."

They both watch another greeting, and this time he now sees a faint translucent ripple of light spiral alongside. Every guest is given lava at first sight, no questions asked. Apollo returns his attention to Andromeda, who returns the focus with a radiating grin. "Tell me, do you know if the Regins would call it, 'leve at first sight'?"

Andromeda pontificates, "That sounds stupid! But I wouldn't put it past them. The way those Regins spout off about it makes me think they missed a few steps in evolution." Apollo thinks about this for a while. How could someone who knows nothing of lava be able to invoke such feelings? He looks around the room, which has been decorated with such lava and devotion. He feels insane for looping around in the circle, only to question whether he might have misunderstood what she was trying to do.

Apollo draws his attention back to Empress Andromeda. "Do you think Cassiopeia will be here tonight?"

Andromeda throws up her hands, "*By Allah, I wish that yin would let herself enjoy life once in a while! Alas, that's not her prerogative. Always at work with that one. I swear this whole galaxy is backwards. Even with this party, she was all business—saying I had to find you, first thing, otherwise the show wouldn't be a smashing success! Trust me, I was not going to pass this up.*"

Apollo feels vain for prejudging the Empress unfairly. She gave him more wisdom in their one conversation than he could remember sharing with anyone in his lifetime. He had unmerited depositions about prana that he was now willing to share with his audience, to reveal to them what he was discovering. Tonight's performance was about healing one's heart. He knew that, because she healed his.

Cassiopeia healed Apollo's heart the way only one who is unconditionally devoted can. She inspired compassion while providing training to her assistants to invoke affinity within tonight's performance.

"Be still my beating heart!" Apollo belts out. His pride got the best of him. He recognized that they both tried to convince the other that their form of unconditional devotion was superior to the other's.

FLASH. "I had nothing to prove, and everything to lose; everything that kept me from Cassiopeia," Apollo pointed out.

Cassiopeia breaks in, "I knew his heart's desire had not been met—because he still pushed his own heart away, as did I. We had such opposing views and reasonings. I was afraid of what I wanted, not being what he needed. With Apollo confessing his lava, I thought I'd try sharing leve with him, giving him space and the ability to call the shots, and never making him feel dependent on me. The more I leved him, the more I only felt rejection! It's humorous to know that both of us tried to get the other to look beyond our words. But in wanting the other to do it, we failed to see how hypocritical we were being about our actions."

Apollo teases, "Speak for yourself. I broke my hypocrisy and went beyond both words and actions."

FLASH. Cassiopeia's image at sunset drifts back to Apollo. "Once my customers see that they want the want, as much as they want the need, I know it's time for them to enjoy their own environment with fresh eyes—and it's time for them to star in their own beautiful play."

The violet seedling drifts out of protection of her tentacles, and all of a sudden he returns to the ballroom, and everyone present illuminated with faint glowing auras of kelly green, sky blue, or violet. He looks down at his tentacles that now pulsate a soothing green. Her voice begins to fade out, "Only then do they give *themselves* the choice to embrace the life they desire; no one else can do it for them."

Apollo spouts out, "I am so blind! She needs me to feel her leve—the same way I feel lava! This is our environment! The words are confusing, but not the feeling. She lavas me, the way I leve her!"

Apollo puts his tentacles on a perturbed-looking Empress Andromeda's, causing her to pull away. "Aye, mate! You seem awfully clingy; I disdain your touch . . . at the moment."

Apollo retracts. "Terribly sorry, Empress, but I think I know what gift Cassiopeia is giving me! She wants me to understand her leve for me!"

Andromeda is intrigued, and leans in. "*Okay, what have you got nesting up there?*"

Apollo responds, with so much delight, "She wants to give me all her lava—errr, leve. I am in leve with—she is in—WE are in lava-leve!"

The Empress begins laughing uncontrollably, so much so that she grabs her sides! Andromeda gasps for air, before returning to a poised posture, "*Oh my, word! Phew. If I was in my phoenix form, I might have burst into flames. Now, you might be onto something, but you went cold fast when you put all your eggs in one basket. Cassiopeia is a professional—she never gets personal with customers. She only creates environments for us to play in as we desire. This event is like a gift box for you. She willed it so you have everything in here that you could need or want; and you get to take whatever you want with you out of this. That is why she hand-picked guests for you to be with. Perhaps that is why she refutes being present.*" Andromeda sneers, waving her arms around, "*She knows how smoldering yangs like you think; she is not a prize to be picked.*"

Apollo tries again, "Cassiopeia gave me the gift of understanding leve from the world of lava. I have to show her; I will make it . . . I will . . ." Andromeda places one index finger on her pursed lips, and really studies Apollo hard.

Empress Andromeda lifts her finger to finally express something she might not have been ready to share. "You know, I have never met a light like you; you are definitely not a fool—yet you are afraid to admit you're ignorant."

Apollo straightens up, "I am not ignorant, I know many things!"

The Empress throws her hand to the side, and playfully asks, "Okay, and for the things you don't know, what do you do then?" Apollo stammers; he doesn't say anything.

Andromeda lets him off the hook, "Don't take that last bit as a jab; I was just making a point. I like that you are ignorant. A fool does not know and does not question. Ignorance is gifted to those who still question in moments of curiosity. It's approaching things even while you're on level thirty as if you're level three. Just because you know things doesn't mean you approach everything like you're an expert."

Apollo smiles. "You mean the Empress admits to not knowing everything?"

Empress Andromeda teles, *"Allah! Of course not! That's why I'm still only thirty-three levels young. The universe would be a more spry place, if we stopped approaching everything with certainty, and instead engaged everything with a genuine sense of curiosity. We need to start discovering our unique patterns. The day I took to my stage, I became aware that not everyone will encourage me to jump off a cliff, because not all are birds, and it can be misunderstood when receiving fowl words if you're a*

224

non-bird-brained being. How was I supposed to know that not everyone was built to fly? It's all relative. That realization freed me from caging my Self. I no longer clip my wings and stay cooped up. I altered my whole galaxy. Try being a phoenix who's afraid of igniting her own spark!" She winks.

Apollo acknowledges humbly, "Thank you, Empress Andromeda."

"Please, call me Andy." Andromeda tosses her hair to the side and teles, "I'm reconnecting with my masculine qualities. And best of luck with filling your box . . . if I were you, I'd think about what life could be like if I'd follow my biggest desires. If you were to shoot for big stars." Apollo realizes his aura has altered to violet. Andromeda is not fazed; it's not even clear if she can even see these auras.

Apollo shakes his head as if given direct orders. "Affirmative. First, I'll put myself in my box—then I'll put Cassiopeia in my box."

Andy puts her hand up. "Woah, Sir Reginald. Maybe divinity has other plans for your lava. You should not force the flow. I think it's obscene that you want to latch onto the first yin that your yang is drawn to." She looks a bit bothered, but calms down. "Last thing Cassiopeia told me this evening: 'First fall in lava with yourself; you'll know what to do then.' I promise you this . . . Cassiopeia is happy for everyone who comes to her in need. Regardless of what they think, she falls in lava with everyone who—"

Apollo jauntily cuts her off, "Well, frankly I consider myself lucky. She does extraordinary things for those who don't even know that they could come to her need. See, we're both writing this performance; I'm just now becoming aware how imperative it is to have this universal shift be a success."

The Empress stands there almost in awe and then teles, "*Wow. You truly do think highly of yourself; and this is coming from an empress of an entire galaxy . . . You know what, I'm getting ahead of myself. This performance is about you sharing your lava however you see fit. Just follow her script, and don't rewrite her play with alternate stars.*" Andy winks; she then continues, "*Allah, I leve beings who try to rewrite history of our star stories, like these annoying huemans named Plato and Julius Caesar; they are falsifying thoughts, misreading planets, and modifying sky stories! Have you heard of this—this thing called a calendar. Foolish Arthlings rewriting—*"

Apollo grows impatient as his aura morphs to sky blue, "Empress Andromeda, I have more pressing matters that trump this—this Arthling drama. I must find Ariyan at once." Really, Apollo wants to speak with Cassiopeia, but being unsure where she is, he intends to find someone who would know where to find her, and might bring them together.

The Empress chirps, "Well, I suppose. We can talk more outside of your box." Before she departs, she holds out her wrist. Automatically, Apollo guides it close to face and graces it with a respectful kiss; he genuinely respects her, which completely catches him off-guard when considering all his lowly thoughts he has built up about her.

This revelation in his altered perspective leaves a coy smile lingering on his face as Empress

Andromeda turns to join the rest of the guests as she teles, *"First fall in lava with yourself . . . I'll be waiting for you to see it through."* Feeling elated, he almost forgets the hurry he's in, he hypnotically nods for several moments after she has left. Apollo thinks to himself about his shift in emotions. Never had he experienced a shift from leve to authentic lava. What bliss.

Shaking his head, he turns his intention to finding Ariyan. Perhaps he is already in the mezzanine. As the time draws nearer to his speech, no longer wishing to hear his internal thoughts vocalized as external conversations, he heads where Ariyan should be now, if not soon, for the commencement. It's almost showtime.

11 THE COMMENCEMENT SPEECH

Apollo bounds up the stairs, and sees Ariyan rehearsing the opening announcements with Julian. Apollo approaches Ariyan with hopes of generating an impeccable first impression, but Ariyan takes pleasure in setting the tone. "Oh, look who has graced us with his presence. If it isn't the self-proclaimed—do tell me if I missed anything, Jules— **'Most honorable being called to this galaxy; Sir Apollo Eirene!' Did I get that right?"**

Apollo breaks the news to Julian, who genuinely nods his head. "Jules, Ariyan is being sarcastic."

Ariyan laughs, "Ah, a quick wit from Andromeda's snake pit." Apollo can tell Ariyan's first impression has already been made.

Ariyan continues, "Ah, perhaps I'm being too harsh on this noble young starlight who is about to deliver words of wisdom about how prana beings need to give up their own righteousness . . . I do leve when hypocrisy gives itself a good ego stroke."

Again, Julian genuinely nods as Ariyan begins to approach Apollo, "After eons of dedicating my life

228

to spreading peace throughout this galaxy, and living out my own practice in my life, I am curious what wisdom our neighboring galaxy has to offer. Or will you perhaps prove to be the voice that lavas peace?" Apollo stammers at Ariyan's massive size close up. Not wanting to seem intimidated, he holds his ground, and looks toward the curtain that separates the audience down below. He thinks of the words he was going to speak, then realizes they don't align with the leader he desires to be.

Apollo feels lonely as he begins to defend his feelings. "Sir Ariyan, to be honest . . . In a non-awkward way, I did prepare a speech full of leve, but—"

Ariyan chuckles. "Don't lie to me; you can't speak of leve, let alone show it. Actions speak loudest. I hope you took it personal, me not wanting to be around you. You clearly don't mind spouting lava to those providing you hospitality, and you permit your squad to reflect the same vulgar behavior. So disrespectful. You're lucky I was not present when you put your tentacles on her. I would've reprimanded you so harshly, I'd have been forced to leave the Peace Department for engaging in lethal combat."

Apollo is a bit surprised at what he is hearing, but feels Ariyan is justified. Ariyan calms down. "I knew I wouldn't be able tolerate your actions, but thank you for sharing your malicious ways with Cassiopeia." Apollo looks at Julian, who seems unsure of him now.

Ariyan alters his tone and makes his way to the curtain, "She really outdid herself with this one. You aspired to be a true passion within her." Ariyan shoots a look back at Apollo, followed by a gesture to have him stand next to him.

Ariyan continues as Apollo approaches him, "You were nominated as their image of perfection—a prana at service in battle. I know what it's like to get respect without anything needing to be said." Apollo stands next to Ariyan and can tell Ariyan speaks from experience; this is not for show.

Ariyan shares from his heart, "You must know, Cassiopeia has earned the same merit as us, but without ever instilling fear into others. We draw legions through taking lives; she draws participation through giving purpose. She does not slay, she serves. She does so without loss of self-gratitude or dignity. She takes slander from the same prana she serves, because she understands that prana only impose their own self-lava and ridicule. She takes the pain and does not refute."

As Apollo hears what sounds like teasing from below, Ariyan responds, "Let's see what was tolerated during your visit, shall we?" Julian stays where he is, murmuring to himself. Ariyan pulls the curtain back so that both can peer down to the audience. Apollo sees Cassiopeia's elegance play throughout the assistants answering questions, and creating light-hearted conversations with guests, assisting effortlessly. Assistants execute all desires requested and demanded by guests. Guests are entitled, crude, and righteous in their ways of acting.

Two of his squad members stand out while interacting with an assistant. From his new point of view, he replaces himself with the two guests, and Cassiopeia as the assistant. He cringes as he watches one guest belittling the doting Cassiopeia, who provides a serving tray and unwavering selflessness. He snatches the food and guzzles his drink, while hastily shooing her away. She smiles and carries on. Similar interactions are all occurring simultaneously, and he visibly sees them. It's no surprise what plays out tonight. Prana see, prana do.

Ariyan summarizes, "Yes, our performances never lie. They tell a great deal about the respect we show to others, based on the respect and leve ourselves. You're like Omega—you don't observe leve, instead you force lava . . . maybe your galaxy tolerates crude behavior, but by Allah, please stop blaming everyone for your own shortcomings. Take responsibility for your own actions; and respect those who turn away from lava, because we choose to spread leve."

Apollo attempts to relate. "I will make up for my shortcomings. I promise to make it up to her. I will never force her to lava me; and I get that I might not have been mature enough for her . . . leve."

Looking off into the crowd, Ariyan drifts off a bit, "I cannot scorn you for harboring your lava. I was once you." Ariyan gives Apollo a side glance, "I too went to war—battling enemies to protect my own. I did so without mercy, only with a longing for justice, until one battle on Fenius. I killed a young yin . . . Sure, I'd slaughtered thousands of yins, on different planets, along with their yangs; but this yin was different."

231

Ariyan looks down, almost stopping his story, but he trudges through. "As the light left her eyes, I saw the reflection of my own yin guardian. With the last glint in her eyes, she reached out to me. My mind was disrupted, as I tried to help her. I tried to help this yin—my enemy . . . all of my enemies. Their lights had gone out as they had fallen. I could not bring them back." Loud shrills and shrieks came from the ballroom floor, sounds of presumed pleasure, but looking into Ariyan's deadened eyes, a specific melancholy image from his past was clearly painted in his mind.

Ariyan proceeds, "I kneeled down among all my fallen enemies who turned into my clan, their eyes wide open. That marked the last day any of us would fight another living being. Never again would they see their leved yins and yangs. Never again would I lay a tentacle on my clan member, from my planet or another, without mercy. That haunted me. Stepping away from that life didn't give me the peace I desired. I started waking up in cold sweats and occasional screams . . . until I saw her."

Apollo and Ariyan lock eyes. "The night before the Universal Network declared an immediate end to any battles due to the War within Worlds, I had dreamt it—I knew it was going to happen. It was some sort of a vision. I saw a misty explosion—I didn't know how it came to me, but I saw it, and knew what was going to happen on Mares."

Ariyan almost became frantic, but regained his composure. "It was a lucid-like vision. I woke up to screams from my spouse, Alpha. I jumped out of bed

232

and tried pulling her out of the dense mist. Nothing came out of the mist, except a lonely young yin. I was caught off guard when she spoke.

"I thought I heard her say, 'I will play when my work is complete.'

"I naively asked, 'What work?'

"She said, 'Not work; word. I gave my word. I'll come see you when I can play.'"

Ariyan continues, "I awoke startled, and told Alpha about my vision. I begged—honest to Allah, I groveled for her not to leave that morning, but she insisted. Alpha openly mocked my validity, thinking my convictions of peace corrupted my sense of rational logic. She took our three obedient offspring to go with her; Omega stayed."

Ariyan takes a deep breath, "After hearing the news of my fallen clan, a cross-communication informed me of a single survivor. While she was being brought to headquarters, I was ordered to greet her, but I could barely breathe when I saw her. She was the face that woke me from my last nightmare. She became my symbol that ended the war within my world. All my repressed lava was released through pure leve. Leve for the yin known as Cassiopeia." He pauses.

"I was once like you, Apollo. No question." Ariyan returns his attention to the performance below. "The difference is I chose peace, and you were forced into it—all because I answered a simple question that most warriors don't bother asking themselves while still thirsty for the blood of battle."

Apollo pries, "What question was that?"

Ariyan looks him dead in the face. "Who is willing to endorse war?" Apollo looks perplexed.

Ariyan grins and responds, "The answer is simple: 'Those willing to endorse war have yet to resolve their insecure battles from within. It's typically for the elite who push the buttons, but engage very little on the front line. It's easy to kill when your skin suit isn't in the game. Working in this building, knowing my heinous acts out there mark me a hero here, is maddening. I feel like a hypocritical poster-child— merited in war, and awarded peace marshal. The title I am given somehow justifies the blood I spilled." Ariyan catches the dumbfounded look on Apollo's face.

Ariyan's begrudged tone returns. "I only heard wondrous things about you; but your actions prove that the Andromedan warriors in service are no better than us Regins. War only breeds one kind of beast— you and me, heroes in hypocrisy. And the war is still so intense within you, but no one can blame you for your trained conditioning. You're conditioned not to recognize that you are fighting your own projected internal battles. But with her . . . how did you not see it?"

Ariyan breaks eye contact to scan the room, "Never have I heard my benevolent Cassiopeia conflicted, wondering if she'd be capable of lava. You've inflicted painful wounds during your stay, almost poisoned her mind. How wicked are you? She will recover, no doubt; she's mastered self-leve."

Apollo sounds delighted, "Did she—I mean, was she thinking about trying to lava me?"

Ariyan cringes. "I do not wish to discuss this topic further."

Apollo grows tall in responsibility. "Forgive me, Sir Ariyan. My intention was not to break my beautiful muse. I knew not what I was capable of; this guilt has been holding me down. How can I undo this? For the lava of Allah—"

Ariyan responds, sounding irritated, "Well, you could start by refraining your use of the divine's name in vain. And you did nothing out of your nature; you're just ignorantly looping a life lesson. No need to apologize, unless you intend on disrupting your actions. Your actions are generated from your thoughts, and your thoughts are generated by who you truly are. Know who you are. Sorry means nothing to these divine life lessons."

Apollo inquires, "How many chances do I have at this labyrinth—errr, lesson?" Ariyan sets his front tentacles on Apollo, and they share a moment of silence.

Ariyan cannot help but grin at this. "You need not worry. It's your game of life. Faces and places might change, but there's no limit on how many times you can repeat a lesson—which, in your case, might be more than others. It's up to us whether we repeat, or finally let go." Ariyan sighs and smooths down his clothing, appearing to prepare himself to step through the curtains.

Unapologetically, Apollo grabs for him. "Cassiopeia is here, isn't she? I need to speak to her."

Ariyan grins while detaching Apollo. "You know, I'm curious if she's right about you . . . why would you need to speak to her?"

Apollo collects his thoughts, not wanting to mess this up. "Okay, I'm not gonna lie, I might not need her, but I do want—I want her to know—I want to thank her for the strength she showed, and the leve-lava-leving . . ."

Apollo searches deep within himself. "I want her to know how incredibly brave she was when I was cowardly. I am appalled that I . . . that I still cannot find a word to express the shift she has caused in my lonely world."

Ariyan looks deep into Apollo's eyes. "It takes real courage to admit to cowardice. Not until you did she admit to knowing of all these emotions she felt too ashamed to share. I did not know she had felt. You . . . you did cause a profound shift that opened her up. I—I do thank you for that."

Apollo attempts again, "I need to speak with her."

Ariyan takes a long pause, gazing down toward the audience. "Cassiopeia is here. You need to speak *to* them, in order to *reach* her. It is time for some courage again."

Ariyan unexpectedly begins descending the stairs with, "I believe you will learn your lesson this time. Be mindful of your audience. They want to be served as much as *you* need to be of service. Perhaps then you will find your lost word, and stillness within your internal battle you're still fighting." Apollo is shocked at Ariyan's parting words. Ariyan leaves, moments before he is scheduled to introduce Apollo.

Julian then pops in, "Are you ready?"

"Allah! You nearly gave me a heart attack!" Apollo seems aggravated as Julian stands in front of him, just nodding and smiling. Apollo dismisses his irritation. "Never mind . . . Is Ariyan going to introduce me?"

Julian shakes his head. "Yeah, no,"—he throws his tentacles up—"that all changed! Ariyan told me that, since I'm Cassiopeia's number two, I'll be introducing you. I was a bit nervous at first, but I accepted the duty with full confidence to razzle and dazzle them as a pre-opening act. Huzzah! I'm not gonna lie, I promise to do my very best! So . . . what'd you say? You wanna do this thang?"

Apollo nods, and Julian dims the lights on the ballroom, and increases the illumination on the mezzanine. Jules takes a deep breath, looks Apollo dead in the face and whispers, "It's showtime!" His face lights up with the biggest smile, and disappears into the curtain.

Apollo runs through his speech, omitting most of it, just as Julian finishes his opening introduction to the audience. Ariyan's voice drifts back " . . . *you've been reliving this life lesson . . .*"

FLASH. Apollo looks at us three, "I knew I was going to speak to her, not from my expectations, but from enlightenment." He clears his throat. "This might have started because of the War within Worlds, but peace was only going to come from us ending the war within words. At this time, I wasn't quite sure

237

about my speech, but—"he looks at Cassiopeia—"I knew she believed in me, and that was enough."

FLASH. In that instant, Julian announces, "And here he is, the most honorable being called to this galaxy . . . Sir Apollo Eirene!"

Apollo steps out, and for the first time truly embraces Julian; this startles Jules, and he inquires, "Are you feeling alright?"

Apollo responds, "I am better than ever. And I know I haven't told you this, but you are such a benevolent being and I am honored to serve with you."

Julian doesn't hug him back at first, but feeling inspired by Apollo's words, he reciprocates it rather quickly, causing the audience to collectively awe. Both disengage, knowing that mutual feelings are reciprocated as Julian exits and Apollo takes center stage. Apollo begins:

> "Wow! Give it up for Julian! He truly inspires me to do better and trust more.
>
> I cannot believe I am here. Only on Mares could an Andromedan arrogantly call themselves, 'the most honorable being called here.' I'm not gonna lie, I would have never gotten away with this back in my galaxy; am I right, yangs?"

A low, roaring laugh of recognition is heard.

"I think the UN might have been misinformed when they selected me. They wanted someone to speak about 'peace of mind'—but what I intended was giving them a 'piece of my mind.' What did they expect, I'm Apollo Eirene!"

The audience is in hysterics.

"But, seriously. I'm really honored to be given the privilege in addressing you all in the celebration of such an extraordinary moment in our universal history. We, as stardust, all traveled on our own journeys to arrive here for one reason: to gather in **celebration** of our galaxies engaging in a universal act toward peace and unity. Peace and unity through trust amongst worlds. As I look around this room, I see no group that is more suited to blaze this trail to ensure this to be a possible path forward.

You all were chosen based on actions that you stand for within our universe. You are the symbols of peace in our worlds. But there will never be universal peace and unity without the desire to understand each other's worlds.

I admit, if it weren't for my Mares experience, in preparation to stand here tonight, I would still be living a hypocritical life. I trusted very little and I lacked any sense of unity. I blocked myself from seeing the equality I shared with you all. Being foolish and full of judgement gave me no peace of mind, and made my world very lonely."

Apollo scans the sea of prana, and without intending on finding Cassiopeia, he sees her in everyone present. He sees her poised lips, coy figure, slender tentacles, and smiles in the crests of every eye; over and over again until he falls in leve with the *whole* room. He hears his heart beating: Bum-bum. Bum-bum. Apollo releases a withheld sigh. Looking down at his tentacles, emanating a violet aura, he speaks from his heart:

"Yes, unity and trust are vital for peace—and no two galaxies represent this more transparently than the unconditionally devoted Sir Reginald and Lady Andromeda. We all know the legacy of these two star-crossed beings. We are their bits that burn brightly eons later. We all know the story, but who dares speak aloud the emotional word evoked so clearly between these two light beings—in mixed company?"

Chatter fills the Ballroom, in recognition and discomfort of the first open conversation about an unresolved, unspoken disagreement between these two neighboring galaxies. Apollo's voice causes discontinuation of side conversations:

"Yins and yangs, there is not one, but two words: lava and leve. It is with clarity I stand here now to tell you—I came to honor a time of peace, by ending the physical war within worlds, now resolving the unspoken war within words. Leve and lava. Our conditioning of universal language must now evolve. I recently discovered that Regins disdain us Andromedans for expressing lava, just as much as we Andromedans scorn Regins for exuding leve. With clarity, I now see that these two words are not complete opposites, but actually very similar. I know lava allows two to embrace and bond. I now understand leve shows affection by respectfully guiding. Both have served us well, so I would like to commemorate this time of unity and trust with the understanding that our words of lava and leve have always been a duality in expressing an emotion that brings us together; they have never divided us. That is what Sir Reginald and Lady Andromeda taught us. The universe is gifting us an opportunity to change our focus. Sticks and stones no longer break our bones, so why let these words hurt us?"

"'I am not easy to lava. They think they are so superior,' I told myself. 'How can they leve so much? What makes them so great?' I asked myself. All these semantics were in my head, causing me to think *lowly* of my Self-worth! Not until I came to Mares did I begin my pursuit for peace of mind . . . and now that I have I found a word to conjoin my two worlds—my world of self-lava with my world of self-leve. I claim this word with a deepened tolerance to guide my wildly roaring flow and give new breath that cultivates growth from which my two words become one . . . in la-ve. Yes, *lave* is what I have come to understand as affinity within different worlds of words. I did not understand the importance of this new word until a conversation with the wise Empress Andromeda, who spoke this message to me: 'First lave yourself, then you'll know what to do.'"

All gaze at Empress Andromeda, who glows with omnipotence as Apollo proceeds.

"Lave can only be manifested once we first discover it within our Self wholly. I take responsibility for my own welfare. We all have an epistemic responsibility . . . to lave our Self and others; universal peace is counting on it."

A portion of the crowd looks disturbed by Apollo's willingness to admit his imperfections publicly, and him asking them to do the same. The majority admires his willingness to expose this, but only a few acknowledge his words of inspiration with cheers. Those who cheer begin to shine bright violet. He continues:

"Lave your unique experience; it is divine. As sentient lumps and lights of this universe, we chose to take this on, whether we know it or not. As sentients, we must not think *lowly* of our laving feelings. We are meant to pursue our own happiness without . . . *lo-ving*, hurting, or hindering our Self or others. I'm not perfect in this practice, but I shall prevail in my discovery. And when everyone practices, we will have peace-populated planets. I know this to be possible, and so do you; because it's happening all around you in this room— by those providing service, for no other reason than they enjoy doing it as much as you enjoy getting it. Ignorantly, I used

243

to glance over them, as if they were mere shadows, not knowing until this event that these prana at your service have occupations and careers outside of this, and choose to be here in their free time. I shine light to these incredible individuals who choose to give themselves freely. There's a noticeable difference between being forced to serve and choosing to be of service. Prana in service are best at serving when they do not feel like servants."

All assistants look deeply into Apollo's eyes with gratitude, while all guests see the serving members as more than just servants.

"Now, I wish to acknowledge to all of you again—for the incredible service you provided out there, but also in here, by listening to me . . . let's see if I ever get invited back by the UN to give another speech about peace of mind."

Laughter rumbles throughout the room. Apollo concludes:

"I hope you honor yourself for your success, no matter what level you are on. From this moment to the next. It's our time for the universe to unite and trust each other—through lave and affinity—

because we are all one peaceful mind. No one is greater or lesser. We may come from different galaxies, but we're all just stardust—all from one beautiful universe. I also acknowledge myself, knowing I have become stronger in this universal nation, because of you all. I'm honored to know you as my guests, because you all have reminded me how radiant I am as a multifaceted being in this universe.

Lastly, I honor Cassiopeia . . . who was willing to show me how to reflect from my sonder light; my world will never be the same. May we all be so magnificent and willing to give the universe our everything and ask for nothing in return."

Cheers are heard from all the violet auras. Apollo lifts his plasma container, and he sees her— Cassiopeia! Tears in her eyes, she magically appears in front of the crystal fountain on the ballroom floor, wearing a white, **fitted dress with a translucent slip hanging from her shoulder cuffs. So simple, yet more radiant** than the Empress.

The room takes notice as they lock eyes. Not a murmur is heard, not a single word uttered. Apollo now understands what Ariyan saw in his vision. Cassiopeia indeed marked the end of the war within his world too; he completed this looped lesson. Her kelly green glow pulsates in sync with his heartbeat; he followed his heart's desire. He chose to be free:

> "I am in lave with her and just realized it. I could have lost her, if I didn't start following my heart. I have learned my lesson.
>
> For all those who pursue happiness, I commend you. There is no way of telling what it will look like, but if it's anything like mine . . . it is to be of service for those you lave. If you don't know who you lave, start with your Self. Yins and yangs, I do invite you to continue this conversation among yourselves, and even into the elaborate feast that follows. Now, let's start this evening, shall we . . ."

All guests hold up their plasma containers in recognition of seeing themselves in what Apollo created through his emotional allevelation:

> "Stay open with curiosity as we celebrate peace and unity tonight with trust and affinity. May we all radiate our sonder lights. Here's to life with lave for our universe; here's to Self-discovery!"

Cassiopeia releases a whimsical sigh, as unanimous cheers and *CLICKS* begin. Apollo slides back, creating an illusion that the curtain engulfs him.

Behind the scenes, an unexpected greeting, "Well lad," Ariyan's voice is detected, "an enlightening performance—given with such ease." A smile linger on the tail end of that comment.

Apollo turns around, beaming with serenity and wisdom. "I found my lost word, and the lave of my universe."

Ariyan smiles. "You know, we're expanding the Universal Network . . . never thought of considering our universe as one nation. Perhaps we should revive this place, aye?"

FLASH. I chime in, "Is that when Ariyan first got the idea to form the Universal Nation and then Spacer University?"

Cassiopeia nods toward me, "That's it. And much later, we got our Making A Difference—MAD—clan branch. It was all possible, because your yang guardian gave the understanding of lave to our universe."

Apollo almost looks worried. "Yes, but sometimes the best intentions do not always have the best results when we can only speak from one point of view."

Apollo looks at all three of us. "I'm not saying you have to alter your opinion, but just be aware that there's always at least two sides to every hand."

Cassiopeia laughs. "Two sides to every story is a more common phrase, my lave. But I've heard it both ways. And you bring up a rather cattywampus conditioned snag."

Cassiopeia looks at Ariyan and me. "The trick is to always have different opinions on lots of different topics; if you only have one opinion on one topic—go find another, and another. Movement only occurs if you can switch points. If you don't switch, your opinions remain stagnant."

I burst in, "Like Sir Egginald before he mood!"

Cassiopeia acknowledges, "Absolutely, like Sir REGINALD before he MOVED. Even if you do not agree with all the thoughts or ideas, understand their differences."

Apollo highlights, "And rather than dismiss a thought or idea, always acknowledge that all thoughts have some validation. Grow in wisdom that different universes might think similar, or very different thoughts than you. Different, but equally valued from their respective universe." Apollo covers Cassiopeia's hand with his, and adds, "To understand and grow in this wisdom will grant you peace of mind. Trust me." I focus on Apollo's smile that cloaks a sense of failure.

I am distracted momentarily as Cassiopeia concludes, "I just wish this cattywampus conditioning was as fun as the word used to describe it." She winks at me, and I sense that even she hides a bit of sadness before she flashes a coy smile. Why does it feel like there's more to this? Why do my duality guardians seem to be withholding emotions?

I ask, "Apollo, Cassiopeia?"

They both look at me intently.

"What's the matter? I see sorrow in your faces."
They both turn to laugh at one another.

Ariyan nudges me. "That is considered rude to say."

Cassiopeia reaches out to me. "You are very bright, Sonder Light. It's really nothing to be concerned with. Just little snagged strings in our lifelines that pop up when we relive these patterns. Apollo and I accept our patterns, and continue on seamlessly."

I offer, "Perhaps I could help with your snags."

Cassiopeia brings her hands over her heart, "How did I ever become so fortunate in life to have been woven within such a rich clan? I am sure these embedded snags will come up soon enough, in another story to be told." Cassiopeia blissfully laughs and gazes into Apollo's doting eyes, "Oh, what is life, but a string of endless stories?"

I turn toward Ariyan, and everything goes dark.

12 ORIENTATION

I do not return to anything. I am suspended in space, engulfed by darkness. Just me and my inner intelligence, which seems to have tapped into a rhyming, riddle type mindset:

> *"Something never uttered, not even one word;*
> *The secrets from Apollo that're simply absurd.*
> *The curtains closed,*
> *The story goes,*
> *But what came after that speech?*
> *What was proposed,*
> *And nobody knows,*
> *To Spacer University, I beseech!"*

FLASH My mind drifts back to my ship. I tele, *"Hello? Was there more to that story?"* Other images flutter in and out of my mind, not seeming to be in any chronological order; several short clips seem to occur on this ship, in hovercrafts, out in the desert, and numerous conversations with Ariyan. They come back to me, rapidly flashing in and out of my memory. Then a clip of the starry sky lingers, more than most.

FLASH. I am standing in front of a cavern . . . I cannot tell how far it goes down; it's a crisp night. My right hand is in another's. They are unknown to me. We are watching explosions in the sky sporadically occurring. Neither of us are frightened. I glance over as the flash of each of these explosions gives me glints of his handsome face. He wears an open-mouthed smile, and his hair cascades beyond his nose. Clumps of hair fly sideways as he tosses his head to the left. I am in a state of tranquility and ease.

FLASH My conscious mind returns back to my resting unit. Who was that? Was that—I think back—Ethan or Gabriel? Why does it seem like my being yearns for that moment again? Why was I so at peace with someone I cannot remember? I do not rise, nor do I care how long I was inside of that memory. I am preoccupied seeing if I can drift back to my previous memory back with my clan. I try to feel for comfort and security.

The friendly Soprano voice returns. _"That's not the purpose of these memories. Even though you can relive them, you should try and just review them. You mustn't dwell in your past for comfort, so—"_

I cut them off, "Well, a lot of things in my past were forced, so I figured I'd try for a change. You got that?" *SNAP*. No response. I try to drift into my comfortable memories, and begin to see an image of Commander's face. A sense of relief comes over me, as I begin to slip back in.

251

FLASH. I jolt at Commander's disapproving tone. "We have to pick up the pace, Sonder. This orientation is crucial for . . . uh, uh—you. Yes, you. You and your proper matriculation development and requirements. Yes.. . . . yes, that's it. And it's imperative *I alone* deliver this commencement speech for the greater good of the universe. Now, what did you have to tell me that was urgent?" My brain is racing. I look around this metal-paneled hallway that is leading us to a single pane of one-way mirror. I'm not sure what I was going to say, and don't want to ask the endless list of questions that are popping up about where we are going.

I remember the one thing I didn't say, "I wanted to say . . . thank you! Yes, thank you, Commander for getting me into this program. I don't know what I would have done if I'd had to spend another Arth year in those silos."

Commander looks anxious, "That's what you had to tell me? That's your idea of urgent?"

Still with little context of this memory, skillfully suppressing my endless questions about this hallway, I smile. "Yes. I think gratitude is an important type of communication. It shouldn't be suppressed."

Commander shakes his head, defusing his frustration. "Oh, Sonder. I cannot keep going easy on you. If you were any other spacer, I'd have to . . . to write you up, or something." We both smile and continue walking. The hallway begins to narrow, and I feel an incline.

Before I say anything, Commander beats me to it. "Huzzah! After you, Sonder." He opens the door, and I feel as if I've returned to a National Park exhibit. I try taking it all in, before asking, "What is this place?"

Commander looks around as if searching for something. "It's the nearest pocket universe. A holding platform; we just have to find our corridor that leads to the Space Program and Celestial Communication Rover. Spacer for short; she's our ship." *CLICK*. *SPACER* is my ship's name! *Wait, why are we called spacers? Is it another acronym?*

Commander continues, "It can host up to five hundred prana beings, and can hover across the entire Reginald galaxy on one tank of oxygen. After orientation, I can show you the cafeteria, study, and your living quarters. Oh! Think about all the wonderful things you'll want to accomplish this upcoming Zero Zone, aye?" It really is wonderful; I can hardly wait.

So many questions and curiosities buzzing in my head. I try mimicking Commander by looking for a particular corridor, but there are dozens to choose from. How will we know which one leads to *SPACER*? I look over at him, and remember reading in MIT that I was assigned to Zero Zone 2045. Is it still 2034?

Puzzled, I ask, "Hey, Commander. What Arth year is it?"

Without hesitating, Commander says, "2034."

I look around the pocket universe, "And we're going away to train, and then coming right back?"

Commander pontificates, "Yes. Which is precisely why—oh! There it is. Come, come. Anyway, it is precisely why it's no big deal that you came with me. And don't let Ariyan get you down."

Where is Ariyan? Did he not come here with us? Is he still angry? I keep walking, shake my head, and return to my train of thought "But Commander, that's eleven years that we'll be gone. How is that—"

Commander blurts out, "Did you ever wonder if asking all these questions wasn't helpful?" I stand there.

Commander exhales, and looks back at me as if he didn't just make that last statement, "Yes, well . . . eleven years is—relative, you see. And well, we do this all the time. It's no big deal. The way these hueman beings sleep-wake, they won't even notice. Honest to Allah, Sonder. You ask such silly questions sometimes. Aren't you excited about what you get to accomplish? You get to help destroy Zero Zone! You and me, kid, we're about to become heroes."

Destroy? I can feel my physical body tremble. What does he mean help destroy? Commander looks briefly back at all the platforms, then back at me. He guides his hand onto my shoulder blade, in a gesture that has us both continue walking toward the corridor marked: AMERICO. What is Americo?

Sounding somber, Commander confesses, "I'm afraid I didn't know what would be best, Sonder. To leave you, knowing we wouldn't be back for eleven years, or have you experience the pressures of public relations first hand . . . prematurely. I know divinity will have it all work out, so I just aligned my trinity with the greater good. I listened with my heart, like your duality guardians would have, and I accepted the consequences." He points, "Now, Sonder . . . Down this hall leads to the Grand Terminal. The Grand

Terminal connects all galaxies at all times to one network. There are many realities happening in there simultaneously, so keep your intention focused on the SPACER hovercraft going to Zero Zone, got that?" I nod.

Commander rests his hand heavy on my shoulder, causing me to slow down slightly. I hear him take a shallow breath. "I'm afraid you are to be exposed to more than anyone should be, at your level; you just allevelated so fast."

Commander takes a knee, and I stop. He looks down the corridor in front of us, then back at me. "What you are going to experience in there is universal truth. What I'm about to say is all true. It doesn't make any of what you know now any less. Do you understand? What you are about to witness is what happens when all truths come together . . . if you choose to always side with the majority. To be part of Universal Nation's Relationships Department, you have to be able to relate with every audience. That's what I do. That's why I'm still the Recruitment Chair for Spacer University. I'm a master at the craft. I always recruit the winning team . . . and no matter whom I recruit for, I always win."

I clarify, "Who do you recruit for besides Spacer University?"

Commander brags, "Why, I recruit for the UN when chair positions open up. I mandate and announce new regulations when they are released by the majority opinion."

I ask, "What happens if the minority didn't know the change was happening?"

Commander humors me, "Well, they should have gotten someone like me."

Feeling like the minority when thinking about my current separation from my guardians, I say, "Do you always side with the majority?"

Commander responds, "Why, yes. To side with the majority is to side with the Universal Net – errr . . . I mean, Universal Nation."

Without too much thought, I ask, "Do you ever consider looking from the side of the minority?" Commander states with uncertainty, "Why would I do that if the majority overrules them?"

I ask, "Well, who says the majority has sound intentions?"

Commander pontificates, "Silly, the majority vote is the most sound! Everyone knows that!"

I shake my head and feel anger rise in my tone, "Okay, how many prana beings are asked to vote in these votes? Do you know the size of this survey group, and who is collecting the data? Because I want to know how many prana voted to rip my clan apart."

Commander seems desensitized to my reaction. "Honestly, I don't know . . . Never thought much of it; never needed to. The majority has always been what the UN says is the majority. The UN holds the vote and decides the size of the surveyed group. So there is no real difference between the majority and the UN . . . Can't they be the same?" I am shocked to be having this conversation.

I respond, "Yes—but not if there's a huge conflict of interest. If the UN somehow benefits over other prana, because they falsify data. You never thought about it? "

Commander thinks. "Well, majority is majority— so, of course I will always side with the UN. Even if it might not always seem like the best choice for everyone, it does allow for everyone to win if done right. I know you like when everyone has the chance to win; right?"

A bit confused, I nod. Commander smiles, "That's my yin! And those Arthlings should be so lucky; the UN used to have them sleep for thousands of Arth levels. They're really not going anywhere; the majority just recycle their prana. While they rest, we will be enhancing them, and by this next jump in enhancements of their technology, we might actually have those foolish huemans out." Commander seems very cold.

But he stands up, and returns to a jovial demeanor, "Alright. You go ahead, I'll be there."

I shake my head. "But Commander, this feels unnec—"

Commander doesn't let me finish. "This is very disrespectful behavior; go now. Hurry, hurry. You better not make us both late for my most thought-provoking commencement speech anyone's ever heard! University is about to be in session." I make my way to the corridor, and away from his face that now holds contempt. I take a deep breath, suppressing my anxiety, before entering the corridor holding about three hundred of the rowdiest platoon members I will soon get to know.

Even with all this surrounding stimuli, I cannot avoid my unanswered questions: What is going on with the UN? How do they have Commander acting like a puppet? Where's Ariyan? Does no one question this unknown majority who votes? What enhancements? And . . . why destroy? Yeah! No one mentioned anything about destroying. None of this fits. There's too many questions. I need answers, right now. I have to know, before it's too late.

I fling myself through the corridor, and into the light. I see prana beings running all around, doing cartwheels and blowing bubbles. This will not be like the pixelated encounters from earlier; nay-nay-nay! This is my time to be seen.

My heart is racing, just as I reach the vibrant room of light and life. Nearing the entrance, I realize I cannot slow myself down. I fly through the opening, dart out in front of a group, just grazing them as I whiz by those by the entrance nearly avoiding any collisions. I whiz to the center of the room and stop, thankfully right before I run through and disrupt the hologram; which has returned to its intense eye contact with me. I reverse a bit, right over Ariyan's foot. I trip backwards in what feels like slow motion. The landing is not as bad as the laughter that cuts right through me.

Ariyan gives me his hand. "Come on, klutz. You're going to make me look like a mook if you stay down there." He pulls me up. I do not break eye contact with the hologram, causing Ariyan to grab my cheeks to shift my stare dead into his eyes. "You okay? You didn't get concussed, or nothing?"

I shake my head. "I'm fine. Who's this hologram, and why do you both look alike?"

Ariyan rubs the back of my head. Sounding offended, he blurts out, "Man, did you hit your noggin that bad? It's Ariyan . . . What, you saying all Arthlings look alike now?" I look between the two of them. I didn't want to offend him, but it's like looking at two Maresans to me.

Me expression causes Ariyan to laugh. "I'm joking. Most of these skin sacks are starting to look alike; running out of combinations I suppose. Relax. Just try to be cool, okay? Stop running around; prana will think you're trying to be too eager, or seem important. And don't seem so curious; prana will think you're trying to stand out, or be unique. Actually, I don't know why I'm telling you this . . . just, be ready to see Arth a little differently, little sister." Ariyan walks away, and I focus back on the hologram of Ariyan. They look eerily similar. It blinks, causing me to shudder and turn away.

It's not until I hear Commander's voice that I notice the floor is flooded with hundreds of spacers. Commander repeats, "Welcome, welcome, Spacer Battalion!" I look around, and stare up. I see all the monitors above my head repeating the message: "Welcome to Spacer Orientation! Destination: Zero Zone!" I look around—the second- and third-ringed railing systems are all occupied by other prana beings. Prana are now coming up from the ramps leading to the dormitories. I hear Commander, but cannot see him. It's not until the lights are dimmed that I see him standing behind me on the third level of the ship.

Commander continues greeting us, as the rowdiness and conversations settle down; then the room becomes dead silent when Commander begins his commencement:

"This will be the year, Spacers. Can you feel the Arthlings wishing to be revived? It's about time we penetrate the Arthlings' barrier that still divides us. We must go beyond the universal language barrier, in order to gain our universal peace. I see it is time. Oh, we have shown them our lave, we have screamed at them—now we will say it telepathically to them! This is the year that we enhance the prana below to go beyond verbal words. I would like to commemorate this voyage trip back into space with the intention to have Arthlings return to their original universal language . . . through the use of our enhands-ments! It is a brilliant form of technology that connects them telepathically so they can tap into the root of lave much quicker. We already have approval, along with the expansion of our program. We will be implanting their enhands-ments soon, and when we return, our little seedlings will have cultivated the necessary desire to explore beyond their sheltered lives beneath their Zero Zone. Our Universal Nation is evolving with . . . with lave! Our Universal Nation that founded this University, and has staffed it with the best sages and masters to help you hone your craft, and become the best spacer you can be when at service. "

The screens show many faces, all in the same uniform. These must be the masters and sage. Do they all follow the majority like Commander? Do they all work for the UN too, or just Spacer University? And again, why are we called spacers? Did they just name us after the ship? A bit confused, I go back to my thoughts on body language. Why would he add another step to teaching lave? This is going backward. Couldn't it be seen as a distraction? Does everyone just buy into this here? I see several of my fellow spacers nodding in acceptance, but I really think this is unnecessary. He continues:

"We represent a movement towards universal peace. What we are going to accomplish in this next Zero Zone is why Spacer University was created. Think of our futures . . . and our future offspring's futures! Think of everything that will come out of this moment in history! This speech is just the first ripple; soon you will be making waves. The universe needs this, and it wants you to be the leaders who are willing to show the way."

He locks eyes with me.

> "Too often, leaders are overcome by their own wants and forget other's needs. I am no better, but I do strive to make it better, by entrusting that those leaders who lead from their hearts will step forward, giving this universe fa chance. A chance at peace, happiness, and lave."

No, Commander! That doesn't make it acceptable to openly shut out and cast away responsibility from those who choose not to lead with their hearts; this only causes more work for those leading by their hearts. I won't play their game. *CLICK*. Oh . . . Is that why Cassiopeia isn't . . . and Apollo? I look back at Commander, who turns away from me and continues:

> "If I am to give this universe the peace that it deserves, I need more leaders like all of you. I need leaders that are willing to go beyond what they know in order to join forces and grow. Leaders who shine hope and unity between misunderstood words, to show it is possible to go beyond their preconditioned truths and see eye to

eye. This universe needs to expand our unified light and lave. I need you all to help build this vision. And with your unconditional devotion, I would lave to give you my blessing in taking this on as a Universal Nation."

The monitors start saying it first, and then I am surrounded by a sea of spacers echoing, "I am of Service." They say it again, all three floors in unison, "I am of Service. I am of Service." I look around, and then look back up as Commander concludes:

"It's high time we stop them from fighting their own yangs and yins. We need to fight harder to have them stop speaking leve—errr . . . love, and start embracing each other with lave. I will stop at nothing. I promise you. With my last breath, I will unite the universe will the language of lave, in hopes of eradicating love; by any means necessary."

Everyone around me cheers for this side of this story. My inner intelligence doesn't seem to like this idea very much. ***"Woah! This is madness. First it was destroy Zero Zone; now eradicate love? Since when do we subscribe to eradicating being justified to bring lave? And how do you eradicate a feeling? And did he say leve at first? Yes . . . I heard him. It just sounds like history is repeating, in the most hypocritical way*** *possible. Why would Commander even say such things? Does he realize what he is declaring? Why would the UN vote for this? Does he **agree with the direction they are going? I do not accept this type of Universal Nation. I want out."***

I begin to exit the room, as the TV screens begin to play images of my protected little blue bubble: Arth. All of a sudden, a dense layer of translucent blankets covers it. Then I see an opening, right above North America. It is now hidden by big letters: ZERO ZONE. Commander booms out:

> "This is our chance to finally free the Arthlings of their non-transcendental zoned planet. We are going to enter above Americo for Zero Zone 2045 A.D. through this hole scientifically called Zero Zone, and then destroy it! This will return balance to the mental and spiritual beings in the cosmos—no longer enslaved to stay in their hueman meat sacks. This year, we rip off their condensed mass conscious layer built of fear and love that keeps them in their sleeper state!"

The screen simulates the blanket layer being ripped off, and the fully exposed planet releasing all its entrapped prana beings. Looking at it, I have a weird sinking feeling that this might not be fully planned out, but I can barely hear my own thoughts with all this cheering. Why did Commander call it

264

Americo? It's America. And do most spacers think that the huemans are enslaved in their meat sacks? If they are, then why do we risk ourselves?

There are so many holes in this logic, and I'm not talking about the one above America. *CLICK*. Did I know about this before I blew up? Do I choose to blow, before they rip off the layer? Something's not right. I shake my head, and refocus on Commander:

> "Let's make this the year HAVOC turns into happiness, HOSTILITY no longer hinders our heroes, and HARDSHIPS get help. Who among you knows how to make a lasting impact? Who is wise enough to make a difference, even for those who are unaware that you are among them?"

In unison, most belt out, "I AM!" This is followed by a few more, "I am!"; then a few stragglers, "I am!" I do not respond, because I am unsure what Zero Zone is, and I am not compelled to remove it just because of a uniformed cult-like chant. Can I really be the only one who sees that Spacer University has become stagnant? Does no one else see that it all seems very one-sided; there is no movement in expanding knowledge? This is all regurgitated!

I look around to see if anyone else seems uncertain. They are all still staring up; no one moves. It's as if I am among a room full of sleep-wakers, all ready to follow orders that come from above. I refuse to look up to receive orders.

I need answers, not orders. What does this all mean—how did I make this right last time? How did . . . or, did I . . . Did I get sent back here? Did I get another chance on this level? Am I in a loop? *CLICK*. My inner intelligence comes back faintly. **_"Come back to your mission . . ."_** I must! Back to the mission! Back to Zero Zone 2045 A.D., back to Spacer University, to the beginning where it will end up, again, and this time, I will finish this loop of history, and no one will stop—

    FLASH. Darkness and silence fills my chamber. I appear to be in nothingness again.

    "Now what?" I ask. "Is that it?" I'm greeted again by a jingle brought to me in part by my inner intelligence:

> _"Here we end 'Part H'; what fun._
> _Lots was said; much undone._
>
> _I hope your curiosity flies._
> _Knowing of these sonder lives;_
>
> _Did you hear it all, my friend?_
> _Her tiny snags still need amend;_
> _Will this story's loops soon end?_
>
> _There's many different narratives;_
> _But surely in one Sonder lives._
>
> _For that point of view, head to 'Part E'!_
> _Back to times at Spacer University._

Will returning to class really do anything?
We shall see; in Everything and Nothing."

ACKNOWLEDGEMENTS

This book was a combination of past experiences, inspiration along the way, and a lot of magic. That's all I can say. Most of the people that made it possible to finish this book I did not know when I first started this project years ago.

For starters, Daniel Janis Ford— you are my most cherished mirror. From the long road trips, group readings, and our debriefed editing session, I would not have leveled up to where I am now without you in my life. Thank you for getting Elements of Style for me and encouraging me to read different author's writing tips. You are an extraordinary partner, and a brilliantly gifted motivator to those who come to you wanting to master any life skills. I love you OODLES.

Heartfelt appreciation out to Annette Binder and Donna Dune! You two are my soul sisters in travel and self-expression through my journey of self-exploration and spiritual discovery; this first book would not have been possible without the combination of your insightful words and constant encouragement.

Along with parents, I'd like to thank my brother Matthew and sister Megan. OH MY WORD—from the frustrations and minor breakdowns that would start out as book related conversations and turn into contemplating the inner workings of childhood memories, or current situations in life, I'm so thankful to have my M&M's always in my corner to keep me grounded, centered and focused. I'm so lucky to have a leo den amongst my clan.

To everyone who helped inspire these unique characters, thank you for being part of this process. In a non-awkward way, some of these characters spring up in this book only after real raw emotional experiences run their course through my life; regardless of how some doors shut, I regret none of them—and I love all sonder light that crosses my path. I am grateful for those who have shone or snagged lines with me, and I truly wish you well. I hope these words bring you clarity, and to those in your path to come.

KNOW ABOUT JANINE AYANA WATKINS

Born and raised in Southern California, but I currently live in Minnesota with the love of my life. I'm a Civil Engineer by trade, but after five years in construction, I traded it in to become an author, fitness instructor, and motivational speaker.

Most of my inspiration for Arthlings, Maresans, and the other spacers come from Burning Man, my understanding of acceptable workspace "norms", and my world-traveling vacations. My experiences, understanding, and exploration within this world have just started, and I am excited to see where this Sonder series takes me and my readers. I'm excited to see and hear what my words will manifest for you and from our lave of this universe as we create ripples together. Safe travels in the universe; keep flowing forward.

SONDER LIVES

Everything and Nothing

Part E

    FLASH. My mind drifts back to the ship; SPACER. It is still very dark, but I turn slightly towards the viewing window and can make out the silhouette of four resting units. *CLICK*. I am still in my dormitory. I draw back on my last memory. *CLICK*. Commander's speech! Was there more to that story? Suddenly I hear my inner intelligence chiming in. It is very faint, but I know the jingle, ***"Every day I get a little bit better . . ."***

FLASH. The viewing window does not alter in shape or size, but the view into the depths of space transforms into a sky filled with billowy white clouds. I approach the window, and appear to be in a high rise building. I avoid stepping on the obstacle of toys littered across the floor, while walking to the window and see the sea. I hear my inner intelligence chime in with the jingle again, **_"Because every day I learn a little bit more."_**

FLASH Same window. Quickly darting my focus around a similar room now riddled with dishes and a sour smell in a much lower level of a high rise. Then my breath is taken away as I witness snow falling. I almost resist myself from hearing my inner intelligence's jingle, because I want to marvel at the snow. But resistance is futile, **_"You might say you want to stay here forever . . ."_**

FLASH. I squeeze my eyes shut, and try to hold onto the ground, but that is when I discover that I am no longer in a home; I'm outside on astroturf grass. As I feel a breeze whisk across my face, I open my eye and beam with joy to see that I'm with what looks like a clan group of five Arthlings all bursting with laughter. I join in, right before I hear, **_"But it is worth it . . ."_**

FLASH. Back in the back music room of the Bivits. Knowing I have the tears welled up in my eyes, I am alone again with no one, but that lackadaisical ceiling fan. I declare, "I will let go and explore." *FLASH*.